Arnold Henry Guyot

Geographical Teaching

Arnold Henry Guyot

Geographical Teaching

ISBN/EAN: 9783742817570

Manufactured in Europe, USA, Canada, Australia, Japa

Cover: Foto ©Andreas Hilbeck / pixelio.de

Manufactured and distributed by brebook publishing software
(www.brebook.com)

Arnold Henry Guyot

Geographical Teaching

KEY TO GUYOT'S WALL MAPS.

GEOGRAPHICAL TEACHING;

BEING

A COMPLETE GUIDE TO THE USE OF GUYOT'S WALL MAPS FOR SCHOOLS,
CONTAINING SIX MAPS AND DIAGRAMS, WITH FULL INSTRUC-
TIONS FOR DRAWING THE MAPS IN ACCORDANCE WITH

GUYOT'S SYSTEM

OF

CONSTRUCTIVE MAP DRAWING.

NEW YORK:

CHARLES SCRIBNER & COMPANY,

654 BROADWAY.

INGHAM & BRAGG, CLEVELAND, O.; NICHOLSON & BRO., RICHMOND, IND.;
FRANCIS RAYMOND, DETROIT, MICH.

1866.

GEOGRAPHICAL TEACHING.

THERE are probably few intelligent teachers who have ever taught Geography, who have not felt, in a greater or less degree, the need of more efficacious methods of presenting it to the mind of the young; for it must be admitted that there are few, if any, subjects of common school instruction upon which the same amount of the pupil's time is spent with such disproportionate results. The majority of pupils commence this study as soon as they are able to read sufficiently well to do so, and continue it until the age of fourteen or fifteen; yet the great mass of young people at the age of twenty cannot state the precise location, on the globe, of more than a very few of the most important places, have very indistinct ideas of the relative population and characteristic resources of different countries, and know very little of the comparative importance of different nationalities. That this is not an exaggerated statement can be demonstrated to the satisfaction of the most incredulous, by a study of the results of examinations, during a series of years, of candidates for the position of teacher.

The reason of this defective knowledge of Geography, we apprehend to be traceable to the fact that this subject has generally been presented to the young as a collection of unrelated facts, each of which must be recollected independently, and each of which, therefore, is very easily forgotten.

It was not until the first quarter of the present century, when Ritter's great mind made its power felt in his remarkable generalizations on the facts given to the world by Humboldt, that it began to be suspected that geographical facts could be reduced to a science, in which hold good the same laws of mutual dependence of cause and effect that prevail in all the other physical sciences. It was much later that the spirit and result of Ritter's labors found their way to the English mind; and it is to their influence, continued and extended by his pupils, that we owe the interest in this subject which is now so generally awakened throughout our educated population; and the demand so generally made by our teachers for something better—some more philosophic methods, and more satisfactory results, in the presentation of the subject of geography in our common schools. The conviction is beginning to be felt that this noblest of sciences has been sadly unappreciated, and that, instead of being a mere catalogue of facts to be committed to memory, it is capable of being made a means of growth to the mind, and of affording the highest exercise to all its powers.

But the question,—How, if this higher view of it be the correct one, is this subject to be presented to the child?—remains as yet unanswered.

It will probably not be questioned that the best possible method in the study of any subject is that which, while it shall give the clearest and most perfect knowledge of the subject itself, shall, at the same time, furnish the best facilities for the complete and symmetrical development of the mind.

To determine such a method we inquire, First, what order of study is necessitated by the law of the mind's development? Second, what is the nature of the subject to be presented, and what is the general plan of treatment growing out of its nature, and therefore inviolable? Third, by what special methods can this general plan be adapted to the needs of the mind in the several stages of its development?

I. *The Development of the Mind.*—Although all the faculties of the mature mind exist from the beginning of its life in a greater or less degree of activity, they yet attain their full development at different periods. They come into full activity not simultaneously, but successively, the full action of each subsequent class requiring the previous development and activity of the preceding; just as all the capacities of the plant for producing leaf, stem, flower, and fruit, exist in the germ, yet these do not all appear at once, because the higher cannot be developed without the preëxistence of the lower as a basis.

The earliest to attain full activity are the *perceptive*, or observing faculties. These through their agents, the senses, are extremely active in the young child, and constitute the only means by which the images of the external world can enter his mind and give rise to thought. Through their use he is able to obtain a clear conception of the general form and condition of every thing of which they can take cognizance.

In simultaneous action with these is the *conceptive* power, by means of which the mind grasps and retains the impressions it receives through the perceptive powers; and is able to recall them, and learns to express them. In a higher development the same faculty is able, by means of ideas and conceptions previously acquired, to create images of things of which the perceptive powers have not taken cognizance.

Next to become active is that *analytic* power of the understanding, by means of which the general conception, which alone could be obtained in the preceding condition of the mind, is separated into its elements, and studied in detail; the knowledge acquired is considered and arranged; and new ideas are derived, apart from the exercise of perception, which are expressed in the form of abstract propositions.

Lastly, is developed that action of the *reasoning* power by which the mind rises to high generalizations, attains the knowledge of general principles and laws, is able to ascertain the causes of phenomena observed, and from known causes to predict results.

We find, therefore, that though all the faculties of the mind act to a certain extent in conjunction, there are yet in the progress of its development three successive stages, each characterized by the predominant activity of certain powers, and consequently by a peculiar character of mental operations. In the first, that of the predominance of the perceptive powers, the child is constantly occupied in acquiring knowledge of the external world by the use of his senses, and through the expression of the knowledge so acquired becoming acquainted with language and other conventional signs of ideas, and is therefore becoming able to receive ideas from other minds through the medium of language.

In the second stage, that of the analytical power of the understanding, the knowledge of others, having now become accessible to him, is added to the results of his own more minute investigation, and finally becomes itself the subject of thought, analysis, and classification.

In the third, that of the predominance of the reasoning power, the mind having collected its materials, looks at them from a new point of view, and, from the study of them in their combinations, arrives at a knowledge of their relations, of the phenomena resulting therefrom, and of the laws which govern their existence and operations.

We may premise, then, as a general principle growing out of the laws of the mind and therefore governing the presentation of all subjects whatever, that the portion of the subject which addresses itself mainly to the powers of perception, and gives only the simplest possible exercise to the powers of the understanding or reasoning powers, is the only one proper to be presented to the very young pupil. This is the *perceptive* phase of his study.

Afterward is needed a more minute and detailed investigation which will decidedly tax the earlier powers of the understanding, and which will give to the *analytic* phase its special character.

Lastly, the reasoning powers are mainly to be addressed; for the facts or phenomena with which the student deals, must be viewed together in their mutual relation and combined action, and generalizations made therefrom, by means of which a knowledge of the laws which govern them is arrived at. This is the *synthetic* phase.

Subjects which do not present material for all these phases can be profitably studied only in particular stages of the mind's growth, while those in which all are found furnish suitable food for it at every step of its onward progress.

If, therefore, any method in the study of Geography is to contribute to the mind's development, it must furnish the appropriate . degree of exercise for all its powers, in the order of their successive awakening; and we must distinguish three natural phases,—the perceptive, the analytic, and the synthetic,—through which the learner in this subject, as, indeed, in every branch of science, must pass in order to receive all it is capable of contributing to his development, as also to obtain a perfect knowledge of the subject of his study.

II. *Nature of the subject.*—We come now to the second part of our problem, viz., to determine the nature of the subject and the general plan of treatment growing out of that nature.

We are instructed to regard Geography as the " *Science of the Globe,* considered, not as a mere aggregation of unrelated parts, but as an *organized whole,* formed of members, each having an individual character and special functions, all mutually dependent and operating together, according to laws established by the Creator, to perform functions possible to no one alone." *

If this be the case,—if the globe is to be considered as a magnificent mechanism, prepared by the Creator with a special form, and a special character and arrangement of parts or members, in order to produce a given result,—then the study of it is to be conducted on precisely the same general plan as that of any other individual organization of which we desire to ascertain the conformation, the laws of its operation, and its adaptedness to produce the result intended.

First is required a general view of the whole, in order to ascertain its figure, the parts or members of which it is composed,— their arrangement, not only absolutely in the whole, but relatively or in regard to each other,—their comparative size, and the general conformation of each.

* Prof. Guyot's Lectures.

Second.—Each of these individuals is to be made the subject of special, detailed study, in order to ascertain its particular organization,—the character, arrangement, and relation of its several portions,—the character of the whole individual resulting therefrom,—and finally the phenomena of life associated with it, whether vegetable, animal, or that of man considered both ethnologically and in the social capacity of states or nations.

Third.—Having ascertained the individual character of the several members, we look at them again in combination, in order to ascertain the influence which each by its peculiar character exerts upon the others, thus to determine its function in the whole mechanism and to arrive at a knowledge of the laws which govern the organization of the latter. Then referring to the history of man, we trace the operation of those laws on his character and destiny, and ascertain the adaptedness of this wonderful mechanism, to the end for which it was created, the education of the human race.

In the first, we find the perceptive phase of the study, since, by the use of the globe, of *accurate physical maps*, and of good illustrations, it can be presented almost wholly to the perceptive faculties. The second is the analytic, and the third the synthetic phase.

What subject so rich in material for the growth of the mind! What other science furnishes appropriate food, alike to the sunny-haired child of ten summers, and to the grave philosopher, whose head droops with the accumulated knowledge of "threescore years and ten"!

III. *Special methods.*—In considering this part of the question we shall direct our attention to the first, or perceptive phase, since, the right stand-point being taken and the right direction given to study, if the final end to be attained be kept in view, there can hardly be, in the subsequent investigation of the subject, any serious departure from the correct course.

NEED OF A PREPARATORY COURSE.

The work of the Perceptive grade is mainly to become acquainted with the form of the earth, and the form, arrangement, and general conformation of the several continents. It is to be conducted by the examination of a globe, as the most perfect representation of the earth, and of maps of the continents, as convenient representations, on a larger scale, of its several great members.

Undoubtedly all will admit that the only value of globes or maps, as a means of study, consists in the fact that they are images of what actually exists upon the earth—that they *represent* the earth, or portions of it, in regard to form, character, and the position, both relative and absolute, of its parts; and thus each, as an object of study, becomes to the pupil an equivalent for the portion of the earth it represents, which portion is in itself inaccessible to him.

If, therefore, a globe or map can create in the mind of the pupil no image of the earth, or of the portion of the earth which it represents, but is to him simply a ball or a sheet of paper with certain lines and colors upon it to which certain names are attached, then it has no longer any value as a representative object; and so far as practical results in the study of geography are concerned, it might as well be dispensed with, and the pupils be taught, as some of us were in childhood, simply to repeat lists of names, headed rivers, mountains, islands, seas, etc. For of what value can it be to a child to know that a certain line on a map is called a river or a mountain range, if he has no correct notion of what a river or mountain range really is? or, that a certain portion of the map is called England, and a certain point within it London, if he does not see behind the map the beautiful country itself, with its farms, its mines, its great cities and busy villages; and the vast metropolis with its trade and manufactures, its crowds of busy people, its palaces, its gardens, even its fogs—whatever distinguishes it from any other great city?

In order to secure the requisite results from the use of a map, we must give it life and significance, so that when the eye rests upon certain signs there shall start into view a great mountain wall in all its grandeur, with its accessory slopes, and its rivers like silver bands uniting them; or certain other signs shall spread out

8

a broad landscape with dark forests, green pastures, and fields of golden grain, and lakes white with the sails of commerce. The child must first be made acquainted with *nature* as it exists under different conditions of surface, climate, and culture; in other words, he must first know the *thing to be symbolized.* Then the *symbol* will have a value, and not till then.

For this reason the course just delineated should be preceded by an introductory course, the purpose of which shall be—by means of a series of simple conversational lessons, and of truthful illustrations which furnish material with which his imagination may work— to create in the mind a vivid *picture* of whatever is most characteristic of each of the great physical regions of the globe : that is, to give to the mind of the child, in regard to each, as nearly as possible, what he would receive by seeing with his own eyes the region in question. These lessons, followed by maps in which the child learns the appropriate symbol for the reality he has been studying, and sees the countries through which his imaginary journey has led him, in their comparative size and relative position, will give to him the correct appreciation of the nature and use of a map ; and enable it to become to his mind, in his future study, a source of knowledge which it could have become in no other way. Having thus made acquaintance with a type of each of the great strongly marked physical regions of the earth, and learned the manner of representing it upon the map, he is now prepared to read the map itself, and seeing the actual country it represents spread out before him on a smaller scale, to learn for himself all the map contains just as perfectly and easily as, having learned the alphabet, he masters the contents of a printed page.

GENERAL PLAN OF PREPARATORY COURSE.

These lessons should commence with what is most familiar to the child—his own locality—as that is within his range of observation, and possesses features that can be made use of in building up the images of remote regions. When he has learned all it is able to teach him, he may, under the direction of his teacher, construct a simple map of the neighborhood, showing the position of every object which he has been studying. A map so constructed will never fail to call up a complete picture of the region it represents. The child has thus taken his first step in geographical study; he has made an intimate acquaintance with a portion of the earth's surface, and has found a symbol by which it can always be recalled, as vividly as the face of a friend by a portrait.

LESSONS ABOUT HOME.

I. *Physical Forms.*—These lessons on the home neighborhood must necessarily be *oral*. Teachers accustomed to give oral lessons, and familiar with the principles to be observed in their preparation, will need no aids in the preparation of these lessons on the physical features of the neighborhood in which their pupils live. Many teachers, however, will perhaps find the following report of a lesson on a neighborhood in Western New York of assistance, as suggesting, better than any set of directions could do, the method of proceeding. The pupils are the children of the farmers of the neighborhood, and the time summer.

Teacher. I would like all of you to think carefully a moment, and try to remember every thing you saw on your way to school. (Several hands are raised, and the pupils, one after another, are called upon to state what they saw.)

John. I saw some men mowing in Mr. B.'s meadow.

Charles. I saw a red squirrel running along the fence by the woods.

Mary. I saw some cows and a colt, and two calves, and some sheep and lambs, in Mr. G.'s pasture.

Fanny. I saw some cherries that are turning red in the orchard across the road.

T. You have remembered several things, and I have no doubt if you should think a little longer you could name many more; but we have as many as we can talk about in one morning. We are going to have a lesson on some of the things you have seen in coming to school. Mary spoke of something she saw in a *pasture.* How many passed pastures in coming to school? (Hands raised.) Mary, can you tell me what a pasture is?

Mary. It is a field where the cattle, horses, and sheep stay.

T. Why are they in the pasture?

Mary. We drive them there to eat the grass.

T. Do they need any thing but food during the day?

Children. They want drink, too.

T. Very well. Where do they find drink?

James. There is a creek in our pasture.

Sarah. There is a spring in ours.

T. (Charles's hand is raised.) Well, Charles, what is it?

Charles. I saw a big crab in the creek when I was coming to school.

T. I thought somebody would remember presently that there is a creek to be passed on the way to school. I am glad Charles has thought of it, though it seems he thought most of the crab. I want to talk of the creek presently. Sarah may tell us first what she means by a *spring.*

Sarah. It is a place where the water comes out of the ground.

T. Has any one else seen a spring? (Hands raised.) Can Charles tell me any thing more about a spring?

Charles. There is a creek running from our spring.

T. James says there is a creek in his pasture.

Charles. (Interrupting.) That's the very same creek that goes from our spring.

T. Now will one of you tell me what a creek is, or how is it different from a spring, since both are water?

James. The creek is where the water runs through the fields, but the spring is just the place where it comes out of the ground.

T. Does the water *run,* James? Can't you think of a better word?

James. It *flows.*

T. That is better. Now I should not say that a creek is *where* the water flows through the fields, but *is water flowing through the fields*. Can any one give me another name for a *creek* ?

Fanny. Some people call it a *brook*.

T. I like that name better, though most people about here say *creek* instead of brook. Can any one tell me where the little brook which flows through the pasture goes ?

George. It goes into the big creek that makes our mill-pond.

Charles. That's Salmon Creek.

' *T.* Does any one know of any other brooks that flow into the " big creek," as George calls it? (Several are named.) Now can any one give me another name than creek for this large stream of water which has so many brooks flowing into it?

Susan. Johnny Brown called it a *river*. He lives in Albany, and he said there was a river there big enough for ships and steamboats to sail on.

T. Johnny called it a river because he had only seen such large streams as are called rivers. You call it a creek because you only know of such small streams as are called brooks or creeks. So we have three different names for streams of water. One of these days we shall learn something about rivers. George, will you tell us how Salmon Creek makes your mill-pond?

George. Father built a dam right across the creek, so the water was stopped from flowing; and it filled up behind the dam, and spread out wide and deep, and kept getting larger and larger, until it came up to the top of the dam. Now it pours over all the time, and doesn't get any fuller.

T. George has told us that very nicely. One of these days we shall learn about something that is very like the mill-pond, but is very much larger, yet nobody ever built a dam to make it.

Fanny. I know what you mean—it is a *lake*.

T. Now we will talk of some of the other things you have seen. John said he saw a meadow. How many others passed meadows on your way to school? (Hands raised.) John, tell us what you mean by a meadow?

John. It is a field of grass.

T. The pasture was a field full of grass, too, was it not? Are a meadow and a pasture the same thing?

Charles. The cattle eat the grass in the pasture, but the grass in the meadow is mowed and made into hay.

John. (Interrupting.) The cattle eat the *hay*, *too*, don't they?

T. John should not interrupt. We know that the cattle eat the hay, but what Charles means is that they are not allowed to eat the fresh grass as fast as it grows in the meadow, as they do in the pasture. Let us try to find some other difference. When you look over the pasture, and then over the meadow, can you see any difference in the land itself?

Mary. Our pasture is a great deal rougher than our meadows.

George. Our pasture isn't rough, but it is swampy.

T. Why do you say yours is *rough*, Mary?

Mary. There are hills all over it and there aren't any in the meadow, only little bits of knolls.

T. But what do you mean by the *hills?*

Mary. (After thinking a moment.) When the ground is a great deal higher than the rest we call it a *hill*, and where there are a great many hills we say the land is rough or hilly.

T. That is well said. What do you say of land that, like the meadow, has no large hills?

James. We say it is *level* land.

T. When you read about level lands like the meadow, you will see them called *plains*. One of these days we shall learn something about a plain. Who has seen other hills than those in Mary's pasture?

Chas. I saw some awful high hills the other day when I was going to Ithaca with father and Uncle George, but uncle said they "wan't nothing" to what you see in New Hampshire, where he lives. He said there were some there so high that if you were on top of them you'd see sometimes the clouds, and thunder, and lightning under your feet, and where you are the sun would be shining. He calls them *mountains*.

T. That is very interesting, and we shall some time learn about those not "awful" but *very* high hills that are called *mountains*. Now we want to talk only of what we have seen. George says his pasture is *swampy*. What do you mean by that, George?

George. The ground is all wet and muddy, and little bunches of grass grow all over it; but you can't very well go across it for the ground is so soft that if you happen to step off the grass you will sink knee-deep in the mud. I got stuck in it the other night when I went after the cows.

T. But how do the cattle get along?

George. Oh! the pasture an't all swamp, and the cattle know where to go; and, besides, they don't care if they do get in the mud.

T. That word "an't" is not a very good one. I should say "is not" instead. Does any one know any other name for a *swamp*?

Mary. Some people call it *marsh*.

T. Do you know, George, why your father takes that swampy land for a pasture, instead of planting corn or having a meadow there?

George. Father says the ground is so *awful* wet—(class laugh) —so *very* wet, that he can't do any thing else with it; and he says he is going to have some ditches dug to "run" the water off, and then next spring he will plough it up.

T. Do you know, Mary, why your father does not make use of his level fields for pastures instead of that hilly one?

Mary. We have some level fields that were pastures last year, but they are cornfields this summer. I asked father why he didn't plough that one too, and he said it is so rough and stony that it is not good for any thing but pasture. The cattle can get enough to eat, and so he lets them run there every year; but he ploughs up the level pastures sometimes and plants corn and potatoes on them.

T. We have now talked as long as our time will allow. To-morrow we shall talk of the woods and other things you have seen this morning. Try to see something more when coming to school to-morrow. Who can tell me every thing we have been learning in this lesson? (Hands raised.) Fanny may try.

Fanny. We have learned about pastures, and brooks, and a spring; and hills and meadows, and a swamp.

T. Now I would like to see the hand of every one who can tell me what each is, and where we may find each.

We observe that in the foregoing lesson nothing has been told the children, nothing learned by them *by rote*, but they have become conscious that they possess a knowledge of certain things, acquired by the use of their own powers of observation, and thus have their attention awakened for future observations and the path to knowledge opened to them. We also find in this simple lesson on a few of the objects accessible in the least varied neighborhood, the basis for the future idea of rivers, lakes, mountains, and plains; while noticing the use of the poorer lands for pasturing, but the better for culture, is a preparation for the future perception of the relation of the physical features of a region to the industries of its people. There still remain to be given lessons on the woodlands, or " woods" as the children call them, in which a simple definition would be obtained by comparing them with an orchard as the meadow was compared with the pasture; and they would be noticed by the children as the home for certain animals, and afterwards their uses to us would be found by them. In the same manner there would follow a second lesson on brooks, in which the animals living in the waters are noticed, and the uses of brooks to us obtained. In many neighborhoods there will be found in addition to these physical forms, various others, as little waterfalls, valleys, etc. All should be noticed.

II. *The Industries of the Locality.*—The lessons on the physical geography of the locality would be followed by lessons on the industries of its people, thus presenting a simple idea of the conditions of civilized life. The following-lesson will serve to suggest the proper manner of carrying on these conversations:

Teacher. We have now had a number of lessons in which we have been learning about the lands, and the waters, the plants, and animals around us. Can you remember any thing which we see every day, and many times in the day, and which we have not yet talked about?

Children. Houses, fences, roads, etc.

T. You have none of you named what I was thinking of, but I think you will find it soon. What are houses for?

Children. For people to live in.

James. We haven't talked about *people* yet!

T. That is just what I want to talk about to-day. Why don't people live in the fields like the horses and cattle, or in the woods like the birds and animals?

Chas. They would be out in all the storms and cold, and perhaps they would get sick.

Fanny. They wouldn't have any place to keep their clothes, and their food, books, and other things in, and they would all be spoiled.

T. Now can any one tell me why people build houses to live in?

John. (After thinking a moment.) To *shelter them* from the storms and cold, and keep their goods safe.

T. We have now found that people need *shelter*, and therefore they build houses. Do we need any thing besides shelter? Suppose you each had a large fine house to shelter you and had nothing in the world else. Do you think you would be very comfortable?

Chas. We would starve if we did not have something to *eat*.

Susan. We would want clothes to wear.

Fanny. We would want beds to sleep in.

Children. And tables, and chairs, and dishes.

T. Let us talk about the food first. Where does our food come from?

James. Father raises corn, and wheat, and potatoes, in the summer; and in the winter he fattens hogs and kills them for pork, and sometimes he kills a cow for beef, and sometimes a sheep for mutton.

T. Where does your father get the hogs, and cows, and sheep?

James. He raises them on the farm.

T. What do you mean by the *farm?*

James. I mean father's land, where he raises his crops, and his cattle, and sheep, and horses, and pigs.

T. That is very well. Now let some one tell me what people are called who, like James's father, have farms, and spend their time taking care of them and raising things upon them, and what their work is called.

Chas. They are *farmers*, and such work is called *farming.*

T. Then it is by *farming* that the farmers get their food. You said we wanted clothing, too. How are the farmers to get that?

Susan. Mother spins wool and makes it into clothes.

T. But are the clothes we wear on a hot summer day like this, made of wool?

Mary. No, they are cotton.

T. Where does your mother get this cotton cloth?

Mary. She buys it at the store with butter and eggs.

T. Now try to remember every thing you have at home that your father and mother cannot raise nor make on the farm, but must buy. (Sugar, furniture, book, etc., are named.) How do your father and mother pay for these?

John. Father always has a "great lot" of wheat and corn, more than we want, and he sells what he has to spare, and has the money to buy other things with.

Chas. And my father sells "lots" of wool, and some cows and horses, every year. That is the way he got money to build our new house.

T. Then it is by *farming* that the farmers get not only their food but their clothing, and all their living. Now can you think of any one who gets a living in any other way?

John. Mr. Brown makes shoes.

James. Mr. Gray has a saw-mill, and he buys logs from the farmers' woods and saws them into lumber and sells the lumber. And sometimes he makes lumber for the farmers, and they pay him for it.

George. My father has a grist-mill, and he "grinds" for the farmers, and they pay him in flour; and sometimes he buys what wheat they have to spare, and grinds it and packs the flour into barrels and sells it.

(Other examples are given, as the blacksmith, the clothdresser, the cabinet-maker, etc.)

T. We have then quite a number of people about us who are not farmers, but spend all their time *making* articles of different kinds out of things which they buy from the farmers or other people. How do they get their food?

James. They sell some of the things which they make to the farmers who don't have time to make them for themselves; and then the farmers sell them the things which they want.

T. Here then is a second way of getting a living, that is, by *making things* and selling them to other people who can't well make them for themselves. Can you recollect any one who gets a living in still another way?

George. Mr. Shaw keeps a store. He buys goods in the city and brings them here, and sells them to the farmers and the village people.

John. Mr. Smith has a stone-quarry where he gets large nice stones, such as they cover the road-sides with in the village.

These two ideas discussed in a manner similar to that of manufacturing, will make the children acquainted with a simple phase of the two other great resources by which the material wants of civilized life are supplied, that is, mining and commerce.

Then a little talk about the work of the schoolroom, and of the church, will present to their minds another class of wants, the supplying of which affords a livelihood to another class of persons. Now a few words about the Constable and Justice of the Peace of the neighborhood, whom all country children know to be employed in keeping disorderly people in order, will give them a first glimpse of a system of government which controls all the people, just as the rules of school control the scholar.

There will, therefore, be found in these simple things with which the children are just as familiar as with the faces of their companions, the means for the future illustration of the whole organization of civilized society—that is, a division of labor in the great business of supplying our bodily wants, provision for intellectual and moral culture, and a system of government controlling and directing all things for the greatest good of every class of the people.

III. *Direction and Distance.*—After these lessons on the country, in the midst of which the children live, there should follow lessons in which they are taught to determine the cardinal and semi-cardinal points of the horizon, by reference to the rising and setting sun. This should be applied by them in determining the direction of each home from the school, and, if the teacher desire, of the several homes from each of those nearest it.

Next would be lessons on extent, in which they are taught to recognize and draw the inch, the foot, and the yard. For practice they may find the several horizontal dimensions of the schoolroom, its surrounding lot; the length, breadth, and height of articles of the schoolroom furniture; the distance of the fixed pieces from each other, and from the walls; the width of doors and windows; and their distance from each other, and from the corners near them. The mile, half mile and quarter mile, pupils learn approximately by ascertaining the distances of their homes from school. It is desirable that they should, if practicable, learn it absolutely by actual measurement; and thus have a correct standard to which to refer distances which may be given them in future study. These lessons on the points of the compass and on extent are necessary as a preparation for the maps which they are now to construct.

IV. *Maps.*—The first idea of a map should be given by drawing the schoolroom. The children have, as will be perceived, all the data necessary; that is, they know the size of the room, and the position of all its furniture; and the size and position of its doors and windows. They have but to determine upon a scale, the need of which they will see from the impossibility of making the map the size of the room; and to be told that the north side is to be placed at the top of the map, etc., when they can commence work. As the map of the neighborhood or school district is a little more difficult, the following may be of value in indicating the manner in which such a lesson is given:

T. Now that we have learned all about the forms of the land around us, and the position of the buildings, the streams, and other things, we will draw upon the board a map that will show how they are all placed together. In drawing the map of our school-room, we found the length and the width of the room by measuring it, and then we drew one inch in length and width on the map for every foot in the room. Let us find how large a country we are to map now. Who lives furthest from the school on the north? (Hand raised.) How far to your home, Mary?

Mary. One mile.

T. Who lives furthest on the south? How far to your home, John?

John. A mile and a half.

T. How far then from Mary's home to John's?

Children. Two miles and a half.

T. Now there are very many feet in every mile. Do you think we shall be able to draw one inch for every foot in this map? That would be impossible. We will draw instead only one foot for every mile. What then will stand for half a mile? What for a quarter? Our school district does not have walls to begin with, as the schoolhouse has, but it has roads on each side of it, and several crossing it, which will answer just as well; for when we have these we can easily put the houses in their place beside them. In what direction does this road, which passes the schoolhouse, extend?

Children. North and south.

T. Mary lives one mile north from the school. How long, then, and on which side of this mark, which I place for the schoolhouse, shall I draw the line for the road?

Children. Draw it one foot toward the top of the board.

T. Now I have drawn it. On which side of it is your house, Mary? Here is the mark for the house. John, will you tell me how to draw the road to your house?

John. It goes south just a little way, just a few yards, then ends, and I go on the State road east about the same distance, and then another road goes straight south to our house.

T. Then how long am I to draw that south road?

John. A foot and a half, for the little turns don't count any thing in a mile and a half.

The road was then drawn, and the house located as before. In the same way was found the greatest distance to be drawn on the State road to the east, and to the west; then the position and length of the little cross-roads leading off from each. This being done, the point at which the several little streams crossed the roads was given by the children most familiar with each. Next the children living between the schoolhouse and these extremes, located their homes; then the public buildings of the neighborhood, the inn, church, post-office, etc., were located at the proper distance from the schoolhouse. Then followed the little groves belonging to each farm, the marshes, etc., the map produced giving with tolerable correctness the topography of the district.

The children may now be encouraged to make at home, under the direction of their parents, maps of the farms on which they live. This will not only have the advantage of giving to the children additional practice of a pleasing kind, but it will also please their parents, and awaken in them an interest in the work of the school. The great value of these exercises, in a geographical point of view, is the practice they give in determining relative positions, in the comparison and estimation of distances, and, last and mainly, in the constant association of the map with the region represented, which is, as we have seen, so essential to the correct use of the map in future. When a habit of accuracy in these respects is thoroughly formed, a great step is taken in preparation for the future systematic course of geography. The child, having thus obtained all his own locality has to give him, he may now proceed, step by step, to form acquaintance with the characteristic regions of his own country. This is done by an imaginary journey, in the course of which whatever would most strike his attention in travelling should be presented in the order in which it occurs, in a vivid and picturesque description, yet in such language as he can most perfectly comprehend. Care should be taken to notice only the striking features of the picture, as too great minutiæ of detail would impair its distinctions and weaken its impression. At the end of each journey, a map of the country, showing the various regions traversed in their relative size and position, accompanied by a rapid review of the main points noticed, will fix in the memory all that is needed, and make the map a vivid symbol of the reality. After the lessons on the United States are finished, journeys can be extended in the same manner to other countries and continents, noticing of course only what is most characteristic of each of these. Thus in England we have the beauty of the landscape, owing to high culture, the commercial and manufacturing industry of London and Manchester; in France the vintage, and silk manufacture—Paris and Lyons; in Switzerland the snow-crowned Alps, the beautiful mountain lakes, and the life of the herdsmen. When all are done, a Mercator's map, in which the several continents and oceans can be seen in their relative position, without the interruption occasioned by the hemispherical division, will complete the preparation for the use of the maps in future study. Then a few lessons gathering together the separate ideas in regard to climate, people, vegetation, etc., in different parts of the earth, making a little preparation for future lessons on those subjects, would conclude this introductory course.

These preparatory lessons should be completed at the age of eight or nine. The pupil would then be able to use successfully the globe and maps as the objects of study, and to enter at once on the course previously indicated.

STUDY OF THE GLOBE.

We come now to the consideration of the manner of studying the globe and maps, in order to accomplish the double purpose of training the pupil's mental powers in the order of their development, and giving him a thorough and lasting knowledge of those portions of the subject to which his attention will be called.

The work which strictly belongs to the perceptive phase of

study of this subject is, as we have already remarked : First, the study of the form of the earth and the arrangement of its great members—the continents and oceans. Second, the form of each of these continents, and the form and arrangement of its great physical features, as mountain systems, plains, table lands, and river systems. To these points, however, we add, in preparation for future study, a few general ideas in regard to its climate, vegeta tion, and animal life, and such of the facts regarding the nations in habiting it as can be immediately associated with its physical char acter.

It must be borne in mind that, in the study of the continents, we are to confine ourselves mainly to what the child can, with proper representations, discover for himself. So long as this idea is adhered to, we are in no danger of giving him what is beyond his comprehension. The only caution needed will be, not to go so much into detail as to diminish the prominence of the great characteristic features of the object studied. These must always be kept perfectly distinct.

Whatever appeals are made to the understanding must be exceedingly simple, the reasoning being always based on phenomena which the child has actually observed; and there must not be too many steps, or successive conclusions, between the premises and the final one.

We must also be careful to see that, whether in the study of the whole globe or the general view of the individual continents, due prominence is given to such of the points considered as are characteristic, and become, therefore, the cause of important conditions or phenomena to be afterwards studied. For instance, that immense swell of land in the western part of North America, of which the Rocky Mountains are the culmination, distinguishes it from every other continent. Owing to this, we have a peculiar distribution of river systems, which, in their turn, create possibilities of internal intercourse, having the greatest influence on the social or national life connected with the continent. All such points must be made particularly prominent in study.

Keeping in mind the nature of the superstructure to be erected, we must so lay the foundation that each successive portion as it rises shall find its support already prepared·; and when, at length, the great vault shall be spread, every pier, every pedestal, every column, and every arch, will be found in its proper position, bearing its appointed share of weight, having its own appropriate decorations, and receiving its just meed of honor.

We must first fix the child's attention on the form of. the earth, and the distribution of the land-masses and oceans. In this, the globe is the subject of examination, the child being told, that, so far as our knowledge extends, it is an accurate representation of the earth. Henceforth it is to him as though he were examining the earth itself, and he proceeds to the pleasing task of interrogating it, until he has acquired whatever it is able to teach him of itself.

After having noticed and described its form, his attention is to be directed to the position of the lands, they being the fixed body around which the mobile portions arrange themselves. He is to notice the arrangement of the lands in two worlds, of unequal size, on opposite sides of the globe—the compact body of the Old World, and the elongated form of the New—the massing of all the lands toward the North, and their divergence toward the South in three different bands—and the consequent converse position and arrangement of the oceans. This is not to be merely a casual notice. The most careful attention is to be given to all these points, because on the form, size, and arrangement of the land-masses depend those great climatic phenomena which determine the conditions of life on the several continents, and which will, in subsequent study, demand his investigation. We thus furnish him the corner-stone for the temple he is beginning to rear. As these several facts are discovered by the pupil he must invariably be required to state them clearly, in his own language, the teacher only correcting such grammatical errors as he may commit, or supplying such new terms as will enable him to express his ideas in a more clear and concise manner.

He next proceeds to notice the breaking, by the sea, of the

2

three bands in which the lands are dispersed toward the South, and the consequent formation of six great masses, which he is told are called continents ;—the smaller bodies, here and there, called islands—the parts of the continents nearly cut off from the main body, called peninsulas—the three great divisions of the sea lying in basins among the continents, called oceans, etc.

This is to be continued until the pupil has discovered, and is able to describe all the different divisions of land and water which appear on the globe, and, wherever it was possible, has found their counterpart in nature. Thus, by the intelligent use of his own eyes, that part of Geography which is usually committed to memory from his text-book, often with sobs and tears, and which is almost immediately forgotten because unintelligible to him, has become an imperishable part of his mind; and the descriptions, instead of being merely a burden to the memory, have been the means of enlarging his power of expressing ideas, and, therefore, of receiving them from others.

STUDY OF THE CONTINENTS.

The pupil is now ready to begin his study of the general conformation of the continents. In order to do this he needs the intelligent use of certain terms to express differences in the land-surface of the continents, and in the forms of their internal waters ; as mountain-range, plateau, plain, river, lake, etc. Ideas of these have already been obtained by him in his preparatory course by an examination of the natural objects, or good pictures of them ; and from these he will form his own definitions.

In entering upon the study of the continents it will be necessary to transfer the pupil from the globe to the *physical* map. He has but to be made acquainted with the conventional methods of representing the different varieties of land-surface, and internal waters, and he will be ready to conduct his own study of the continent, just as he previously did that of the globe.

As many different points will now require notice, it is indispensable that we endeavor to ascertain the logical order in which to present them, that is, the order of their successive dependence. To do this let us select any single point, as that of climate, and inquire by what it is influenced, and what it does control.

The most general influence bearing upon the climate of a continent is the position of the latter in reference to the poles, by which it is exposed to the more or less direct rays of the sun. Next is its contour,—determining the position in which the sea winds strike it, —its size, determining the comparative extent of their influence upon it, and the position of its great lines of elevation, whether so as freely to admit these winds, or entirely to shut them out from the main body. The arrangement of the surface also determines the combination and distribution of the internal waters, which, because so intimately connected with the former, should immediately follow it. The study of these points then, properly, should precede that of the climate, in order that when it is taken up the child may not be obliged to remember the facts concerning it as mere isolated statements, but being led by a simple association of the phenomena with their cause (the philosophic relation, in its full extent, cannot, of course, be given him), he will have them stored in their proper niche, where they will always be found when demanded.

Again, on the soil and the climate depends the general character of the vegetation in different portions of the Continent. On the vegetation depends the presence or absence of certain classes of animals which subsist on vegetation. On the presence in different parts of the continent of such plants or animals as are necessary to his subsistence, depends the existence of man, if in an uncivilized condition ; and the differences in the surface, soil, climate, and the distribution of vegetation, animals, and minerals, in the different portions, will necessarily give rise to different industries, different social conditions, and different degrees of advancement in the civilized state ; that is, to differences in regard to the possibility of the presence of great nationalities in different portions of the continent.

If evidence is needed in relation to the influence of physical conditions on the industrial pursuits, and distribution of population, we have but to look at our own country.* In the Northeast, the rough surface, the somewhat sterile soil, and the cold climate, make agriculture impracticable in the larger part of the country, while the abundant water-power, and the rich stores of coal and iron, make it the great workshop of the nation. Its fine harbors, capable of receiving and sheltering the ships of all nations, make it also our commercial depot. Hence it is that the greater part of the manufacturing and the foreign commerce of the country is carried on by the few States north of the Potomac.

Again, the level surface making cultivation easy, the fertile soil, and the warm and moist climate producing a luxuriant vegetation, make the great plains of the interior and the South the nation's farm and garden, from which, were its resources fully developed, supplies might be drawn capable, one might almost say, of feeding the world, and, with the aid of the Northeast, of clothing it. In these two regions are gathered almost the entire population of the country.

The great plateau of the Rocky Mountains, on the contrary, doomed, in almost every part, by its saline soil and its want of moisture, to hopeless sterility, is incapable of supporting a population, and must have remained uninhabited but for the rich mineral treasures embosomed within it. Its population, however numerous it may become, must be mainly confined to the single occupation of mining; and will be dependent for daily bread upon the East, or the fertile valleys beyond the Sierra Nevada, which enjoy all the moisture that but for this great barrier would have been dispersed over the whole.

We find, therefore, growing out of the successive dependence, the following order of topics:

1. Position on the Globe.
2. Size and Contour.
3. Surface (Relief) Elevation.

* See Guyot's Maps, in which the differences in surface are indicated by difference in color.

4. Internal Waters.
5. Climate.
6. Vegetation.
7. Animals.
8. Races of People.
9. Distribution, industries, social organization, intellectual condition, and history of the civilized inhabitants.

The last, the distribution of man in the social capacity of States or nations, constitutes that department of the subject called Political Geography, the one which is usually first presented to the young, and, in fact, the only one presented to any extent.

This, it must be conceded, cannot be *intelligently* studied until a knowledge has been acquired of the physical conformation, the soil, the climate, the resulting vegetable and associated animal life, which make the possibility of the presence of civilized States or nations in one part of the continent while they are absent from another. If the facts concerning their distribution be given the pupil before he has any idea of those physical conditions which govern it, though he may remember them, they will be of little worth to him, because he does not receive them in their proper connection, and cannot study them intelligently as the result of causes with which he is familiar—whose influence even he can perceive if his attention be directed to it—but they are to him simply isolated facts to be remembered, awakening no thought and stimulating to no further study.

We have seen that this topic of political geography belongs properly to the analytical phase of the subject. It must, therefore, be very sparingly presented in the *perceptive* portion. Only the *most prominent facts*, and such as are most *obviously* and *unmistakably traceable* to the great physical characteristics of the continents, can be presented; and even these must be given only *after* the preceding topics are thoroughly known, so that the pupil can himself trace the relation of the one to the other.

In this study of the continents, accurate physical maps are *indispensable*; and, if possible, they should be entirely free from all lines or colors in licating arbitrary political divisions, as these can but mar the distinctness, and break the unity of the all-important physical features.

The child must see only the divisions and limits which Nature made, if he is to gain a correct idea of her work.

The first of the topics enumerated above (Position on the globe) the pupil has considered in his examination of the globe, and it needs simply to be recalled. In the next three, which constitute the main work of this grade, the same general course is pursued as in studying the globe. That is, the pupil is to discover, by the use of his own eyes, what exists, and give correct expression to the facts which he discovers.

One very important addition is, however, to be made. The pupil must invariably construct maps of the country he is studying. When upon the *contour*, his map will show only the outline; when upon the *surface*, the mountains and other elevations must be added in their place; and when upon the *internal waters*, these must appear. In all these exercises the closest accuracy must be required.

There are several reasons why this drawing should be insisted upon. First, it aids, by the closer and more minute observation required than is necessary for a simple description, to fix the physical features in the memory. Second, it affords a variety of exercises, by means of which the attention can, without weariness, be kept on these all-important points for a greater length of time. Third, it cultivates a power of representation which will be invaluable to the pupil in future study; and lastly, at no after period in his life can he so easily acquire facility in this representation as now, and be so easily interested in the many little details which are necessary to accuracy. He takes delight in examining the minute peculiarities of contour and relative position; and what the older pupil would neglect as unimportant and wearily stupid, the child of nine years considers worthy of the greatest attention and the most prolonged effort.

STUDY OF THE MAP OF NORTH AMERICA.

Suppose that the Continent of North America is to be the subject of study, and that the several points enumerated above * are to be treated in such a manner as to secure to the pupil a thorough and accurate knowledge of the leading facts in regard to each, and at the same time, to give the greatest amount of training which they can afford to his powers of mind.

In order to secure the latter object, we establish for ourselves this rule : *Tell the pupil nothing which, by a reasonable effort, he can ascertain for himself.* We thus at once shut ourselves out from that, to the indolent and ignorant teacher, delightful plan of assigning a lesson in the text-book, and requiring the children to commit it to memory and recite it by rote.

Let us proceed now to ascertain how much of the material ordinarily given in text-books on Geography the pupil of average intelligence, under the guidance of a skilful teacher, can discover for himself by no more than a perfectly reasonable and healthful exercise of his powers ; provided always, that the proper instrumentalities, in the form of a globe, and a *correct physical map* of the continent, be given him.

POSITION.—The teacher places the globe before the pupil and asks him to examine it, and ascertain the *position* of North America, his attention being directed to the following points : 1. The *World* to which it belongs. 2. The *Hemisphere* in which it is situated. 3. Its position in regard to the surrounding oceans, and its connection with other continents. A little examination will supply the needed facts, which the pupil should give in a connected description of the position of this continent, something like the following : "North America is the Northern Continent of the New World. It lies wholly in the northern Hemisphere, its southern point extending nearly to the equator, and its northern far toward the pole. It lies between the Atlantic and the Pacific Ocean ; has the Arctic Ocean on the north, and is connected to South America by the Isthmus of Panama."

* See page 27.

CONTOUR.—When the teacher is sure that all have remarked the position, and accept the description as a correct one, he sets aside the globe, and places before the class Guyot's Physical Map of the Continent, asking them to notice the number and comparative lengths of the great coast lines. They find that there are three, the western of which is much longer than the others. He asks what name we give to a three-sided figure.* What may we say of the form of North America, since it resembles a triangle? Which is the broadest part of the continent? Which the narrowest? Some one is now required to find the most western, the most eastern, and the most southern points. The names of the three extreme points, Cape Prince of Wales, Cape Charles, and Punta Mariato, are now given. The several ideas gained are now put together by the pupil in a connected description. He says: " North America is triangular in form, having its longest side at the west. It is broadest in the northern part, and is very narrow and pointed at the south. Its most western point is Cape Prince of Wales, at the junction of the Arctic and the Pacific coast ; the most eastern, Cape Charles, joining the Arctic and the Atlantic coasts ; and the most southern is Punta Mariato."

The different coasts are now compared in regard to their *indentations* and *projections*. The pupils notice that the long line of the Pacific coast is almost unbroken, while the two shorter coasts are each broken by an immense Mediterranean extending far into the interior of the continent, and by small peninsulas projecting far into the ocean. They notice also the proportions of different parts of the coast lines. For instance, the part east of Hudson Bay is about one-third the entire Arctic coast ; Cape Mendocino divides the Pacific coast into two nearly equal parts ; the Atlantic coast, continued to a junction with the Pacific, is divided by the entrance to the Gulf of Mexico, and the various projections outside the general line of the coast, into nearly equal parts. Thus, one after another, all the details of the form are noticed and described by the children.

Now, in order to secure more minute observation, to fix the

* The children are supposed to know the terms *triangle* and *triangular*.

31

attention longer, and thus impress these peculiarities of form more clearly and firmly upon the mind,—the pupils are required to draw the outline of the continent, and while so doing, to learn the name of every important indentation, projection, and island along each coast. When this is done, they may gather all the different facts noticed, into a correct description of each coast, noticing first, its direction; second, its indentation; third, its projections; fourth, its islands. Thus: "The Atlantic coast extends from northeast to southwest. It is broken in its southern part by the great Mediterranean, called the Gulf of Mexico. Its principal smaller indentations are the Gulf of St. Lawrence, Delaware and Chesapeake Bays, Albemarle and Pamlico Sounds. Its principal projections are Nova Scotia, Cape Cod Peninsula, and Florida.* The most prominent capes are, Cape Sable of Nova Scotia, Cape Cod, Cape Hatteras, Cape Sable of Florida, and Cape Catoche. The principal islands off this coast are, Newfoundland, at the entrance to the Gulf of St. Lawrence; Prince Edward's Island, in this Gulf; Long Island, southwest of Cape Cod; the Bahamas, east of Florida; and the West Indies, at the entrance to the Gulf of Mexico."

Besides these connected descriptions of each coast, which are given by the children, there may be a third exercise in naming and describing the position of all the important points on the map, after the usual mode of map questions. A fourth and very valuable exercise is that of sketching rapidly each day, in the presence of the class, so much of the map as they have already mastered, requiring them to name each object *immediately* upon its appearance on the blackboard. We have thus four different map exercises: First, drawing the outline and learning names; Second, forming connected descriptions of each coast; Third, recitation from ordinary map questions; Fourth, rapidly naming all the important points while the map is being sketched. This variety of exercises will enable us pleasantly to occupy the children upon the study of the map, until all they need to know in regard to the general form and

* Yucatan, though a peninsula, is not a *projection* beyond the general line of the coast, but forms a part of it.

2*

contour of North America is indelibly fixed upon the memory; while the constant and minute observations required in the first and fourth, and the exercise in the formation of correct description in the second and third, will have given a very valuable training to their powers of perception and expression.

A. *General Study of Surface.*—We have now completed all that appertains to the external form or figure of the continent. We are next to study its internal conformation, that is, the form and arrangement of its parts.

To prepare for this study, the teacher recalls the terms used in speaking of different varieties of surface, asking what difference we have noticed between the land surface of the earth and the surface of the sea. (The former higher in some parts than in others,—the latter uniform.)

What classes of high lands have we? "Mountain ranges and table lands." What of low land? "Valleys and plains." What is the difference between a mountain range and a table land? "A mountain range is a narrow *ridge or wall* of high land extending across the country; while a table land is a broad, extended surface of high land." What between a valley and a plain? "A valley is a narrow band of low land between higher lands, while a plain is a broad extent of low lands." When these distinctions are made perfectly clear by the aid of natural examples familiar to the children, or of good pictures, the teacher explains the manner of indicating upon the map these different varieties of land surface. Thus: "The low lands, whether they are valleys or plains, are colored *green*. Now let some one go to the map and show me all the plains of North America. The table lands, or high plains, are colored a uniform light brown like this,"—(pointing to the color in the map). "Now let some one show me all the table-land surface of North America." "The mountain walls are represented by a double band of dark brown waving lines like this,—(pointing to a mountain range). The higher the mountains are, the darker and wider is the band which represents them; and in those which are very high, so that their tops are sometimes covered with snow throughout the year, the middle of the band is left white. The low mountains, or ridges of hills, have only very light narrow bands to represent them; while a single slope or step, called a *terrace*, descending from the higher part of a plain or a table land to a lower, has a single band or shading of the same kind." After stating how each of these objects is represented, the teacher will, as in regard to the plains and table lands, call upon the pupils to find mountain ranges, high mountains, lower mountains, hills, terraces, the highest mountains in the continent, the longest mountain range, etc., until perfectly sure that every pupil knows what each of these signs indicates.

"These uniform blue spots on the map represent lakes, these black waving lines are rivers; and these parts of the map, along the coast or rivers, which are covered with blue lines, are marshes. Now let some one find all the large lakes in North America, another the largest river, another a marsh, etc."

Thus the pupils are drilled in the alphabet of the map. Now commences the work of mastering the internal structure, which is conducted in the same manner as was that of studying the contour—by mapping, connected with descriptions formed by the children, and the other exercises heretofore indicated. The children should have in readiness upon their slates, a blank outline of the continent, one being also upon the blackboard with the printed map hanging beside it. Some child is now sent to find upon the printed map the longest continuous mountain wall, and to describe its position in order that the class may know precisely where to draw it.

Its name being given him, he says: "The longest mountain system of North America is that of the Rocky Mountains, which extends through the western part of the continent, from the Arctic Ocean nearly to the Gulf of Mexico. It is continued southward to the Isthmus of Panama by terraces." A question or two will be needed to call attention to the distance of these mountains from the Pacific, and their few important changes in direction. Some one may now be required to draw them in their proper place in the outline upon the blackboard, while the rest draw them upon their slates. If the work on the blackboard is accepted by the class as correct, some one is bidden to find the system next in extent, which is treated in the same manner. We proceed in this manner day by day until the pupils have learned the names and position of all the important mountain systems, lakes and rivers, in the continent. In recitation a blank outline is again upon the blackboard; but the printed map is rolled up, and the pupils are required, without its aid, to draw in the proper place and describe the position of each of the several objects called for by the teacher. A *perfect* recitation will be the accurate description of the position, and the correct drawing, *from memory*, upon the blank map, of so many objects as were, on the previous day, examined upon the printed map. By the same variety of exercises which was employed in learning the contour, we keep the attention on these all-important points,—the arrangement of the surface and the internal waters,—until they are perfectly mastered. The minute and constant observation required in order to the accurate drawing, from memory, of all parts of the structure, will have engraved the continent in an indelible picture upon the mind of the pupil; and will have given him, in regard to it, a clearness and precision of knowledge which could have been secured in no other way.

B. *Distinct Regions forming the Continent.*—The various features of the surface of the continent have thus far been regarded separately, and studied only in reference to their position and extent. The continent has been considered as a single mass, having certain peculiarities of surface. Now we look at it in a new point of view. We group together, in their natural order, those individual features of surface, and thus find that the continent is not a single mass, but is a compound individual consisting of distinct parts, each of which is not a fragment, but is in itself a lesser whole, having a conformation peculiar to itself, and which we must eventually study separately.

Some pupil is asked to find on the map the greatest region

of high lands upon it. He says: " A great highland region fills al. the western half of the continent, extending from the Arctic Ocean to the Isthmus of Panama." Another is required to find that which is next in extent. He says: "A smaller highland region lies in the eastern part of the continent, extending from Cape Charles nearly to the Gulf of Mexico." Another is called to find the greatest region of plains. He indicates several great plains in the interior of the continent. The teacher tells him that the bands of light brown which cross the interior of the continent are but very little higher than the parts colored green. They, compared to the great highlands the east and west of them, are also lowlands; and we may, therefore, consider the whole interior of the continent as one great plain. Of how many parts, therefore, does the continent of North America consist? The pupils at once say, " The continent of North America consists of three parts,—a great highland region on the west, a smaller one on the east, and a great plain between."

We are now to study the continent in its vertical dimensions. We no longer consider it as being simply surface, but must regard it as a solid—as having height as well as length and breadth. This conception of the continent as a solid must be made clear to the pupils, for upon this fact, and the differing elevations of the different portions, depends the entire distribution of the systems of internal waters, and many of the climatic conditions, particularly that of moisture.

In order to give this idea, we must turn the attention for a moment away from the printed map to some representation which shall show vertical dimensions instead of horizontal. In the absence of relief maps, recourse must be had to the profiles which are placed at the bottom of the map; and the use of these must be prepared for by an explanation something like the following, though the teacher's own ingenuity may devise a better, and may suggest many expedients to aid the pupil's imagination in grasping the idea.

" In looking at the map we see the different parts of the continent as we might see them if we could be lifted up into the air, and look down upon the whole of it at once. We see how the different parts are placed together to make the continent; and we see the length and breadth of each, and can compare them in regard to size. But the continent has more than length and breadth. It has height also, and it is necessary for us to know how the different parts compare in regard to height. This we cannot learn by looking down on the continent from above, for all parts then appear of the same height. We must be able to look against the continent from one side, and thus see the broken line which we should make in travelling across its surface, just as in looking against a mountain range we see the broken line which its summit makes against the sky.

"The surface of the sea forms the smooth, uniformly rounded surface of the globe; and the continents, which rise above the level of the sea, break its smooth, evenly curved surface, just as those large rough knots or bunches on the rind of an apple break its smooth surface. We might pare all these knots carefully away, and leave the apple perfectly smooth and round. In the same way, we may suppose that we pare away the continents from the curved surface of the globe, leaving it evenly rounded in all parts, just as the surface of the sea now is. Now, if we could take one of these continents which has been carefully pared off from the globe, just as we can take this knot from the apple, and cut down through it from top to bottom thus (suiting the action to the word), and take away the one part, we could look against the other part and see how it varies in height from side to side, which parts are the highest, and how much higher one part is than another. This drawing at the bottom of the map (Profile B to B') shows us how the continent of North America would appear to us, if we could thus pare it away from the globe, at the level of the sea, and divide it along the black line, which you see here (pointing to it) crossing the map.

"The bottom of this drawing, which is a straight line, is the level of the sea, or, as we might call it, the bottom of the continent. The upper line of the drawing is the line which the top or surface of the continent would make against the sky if we could place it before us, and see it as you see this divided knot from the apple. In crossing the continent here, from east to west, we would be obliged to ascend and descend, as this line does." The teacher now follows with a pointer the surface line of the profile, while some pupil follows the line on the map, pointing to each object as the teacher speaks of it. The teacher says: "Here, at the Atlantic coast, the land is, as you see, just at the level of the sea. Now as we go westward, it rises gently higher and higher until we reach the summit of the Appalachian mountain system. Each of these little points is one of the ranges of this system, and the hollows between them are the valleys which separate those ranges. Beyond these mountains the land descends gently until we reach the Mississippi River, where it is again not far above the level of the sea. We cross the Mississippi, and at once the land begins to rise agniu, and continues gently to become higher and higher, until we reach this terrace* toward the Rocky Mountains. Here, as you see, the plain has become a table land, and is as high as the summit of the Appalachian Mountains. From this point it rises very rapidly, until at the foot of the Rocky Mountains it is twice as high as the Appalachian Mountains. Here rises that great wall of the Rocky Mountains, which we see is much higher than any other part of the profile; so high, that all this upper part is constantly covered with snow. The second range, though much lower, is still very high, and so is also the narrow valley between the two. These mountains, we see, are on the highest part of the great table land. From this point it descends very gently toward the west. In crossing it we find the Wasatch Mountains, the Humboldt River Mountains, and the Blue Mountains, which, although they extend so far above the level of the sea, are but little higher than the surface of the table land on which they rest. Now we find the great wall of the Sierra Nevada Mountains which rise from the western border of the table land. Beyond this the land descends rapidly to the level of the sea, its slope being broken only by the low Coast Mountains.

* About longitude 100°.

" Thus you see that from the Atlantic the surface of the continent ascends gently to the Appalachian Mountains, remains at nearly a uniform level across them, then descends to the Mississippi, which is not much above the sea level. Now it ascends again to the foot of the Rocky Mountains, remains at nearly the same height to the Sierra Nevada, and then descends again to the sea level.

" Now of what does the Continent of North America consist? "
" Of two highland regions with their slopes,—the western very large and very high,—the eastern much smaller and lower."
" Where is the great plain which we see on the map?" " That is only the lowest part of the long, gentle inner slopes of these highlands, which descend nearly to the level of the sea."

We must tell the pupils that this great plain formed by the lower part of these two slopes is very different in some respects from their high parts near the mountains ; and that, therefore, we shall be obliged by and by to study it separately. For this reason we will give it a separate name. They will readily suggest the names Pacific Highlands, Atlantic Highlands, and Great Central Plain, as appropriate ones for these regions, on account of their several positions.

The plain may be considered as terminating westward at the terrace along the 100th meridian, beyond which line the increase in height becomes more rapid and the character of the country becomes entirely different, as we shall see further on.

C. *Study of individual parts composing the Continent.*—The study of these regions as separate individuals now commences This is conducted by reference to the map for the position and comparative extent of each ; and to the profiles for their general conformation and comparative heights. A few judicious questions, directing attention to these several points, will result in the pupils forming a description of the Pacific Highland region something like the following :

" The Pacific Highlands form the entire western half of the continent. They extend from the Arctic Ocean to the Isthmus of Panama, and are broadest in the central portion, where they extend from the Pacific to the middle of the continent. This region consists of a great table land, with the Rocky Mountain system resting upon its eastern and highest portion, and the Sierra Nevada and Coast system on its western border. Both systems, continued on the south by terraces, extend throughout its entire length. The ranges are highest in the middle and broadest part of the table land, though the highest peaks are in Mexico. The table land gradually increases in height from the Arctic Ocean southward to Mexico, where it is highest; then it descends rapidly to the isthmus. Throughout its whole extent to Mexico it is nowhere broken by any low lands crossing it, but is one great continuous mass,—the *roof* of the continent." In a similar manner the pupils will readily form appropriate descriptions of the other regions. Their attention must be called to the remarkable difference in extent and height between the two highlands; and to the fact that while the immense mass of the western, stretching from one extremity of the continent to the other, is entirely unbroken, so that there is nowhere any natural passage from the Pacific to the interior,—the lower eastern highland is entirely broken through in its northern part by the great valley of the St. Lawrence; and in its central by that of the Hudson and Mohawk. They are led also to remark that this highland, instead of extending southward to the extremity of the continent, as does the western, is cut off midway in its course by that great depression through which the waters of the ocean penetrate into the heart of the continent. Thus by the intelligent use of their own eyes the pupils have learned from the map, with ease and pleasure, what, if placed in their hands to be learned from a book, would have been entirely uninteresting and unintelligible to them, and would have been acquired with the greatest difficulty. How many teachers have groaned in spirit over the difficulty of getting the children to learn and remember even the simple descriptions of the surface of North America which are usually given in common school geographies! Here all the leading facts contained in such descriptions have become known to them; they have formed the descriptions themselves; and a few minutes' study in any book where these facts are gathered in a proper order, with the few additional details which are of importance, will be all that is needed to secure an admirable recitation—admirable in the readiness and pleasure with which it will be conducted by the pupils; and still more admirable in the fact that they are giving expression to their own ideas, the results of their own thought and research, instead of simply repeating, parrot-like, the words of another mechanically committed to memory, soon to be forgotten, and entirely useless to them.

D. *Distribution of Internal Waters.*—In examining the distribution of the internal waters, while we guide the pupil in grouping the individual rivers and lakes into systems distinct one from another, we at the same time begin the exercise of his reasoning power in considering the *cause* of such a distribution of waters as he finds to exist. Here the greatest caution is needed; for in the first place, the child is capable of only the very simplest processes of reasoning, such as might almost be considered as rather the *association* of related facts, than the tracing of the influence of one upon the other as cause and effect. Second, we must guard against forming habits of illogical reasoning, or of reasoning from questionable data. We must, therefore, confine ourselves to the presentation of the simplest and most evident relations between the arrangements of surface and the distribution of the internal waters, such relations as no child of average intelligence can fail to seize; and we must be sure that the data on which the reasoning proceeds is *true*, established beyond the shadow of doubt; and that the relation we would lead him to discern is not simply a coincidence, but is unquestionably one of cause and effect. Whatever pet theories in regard to these matters we may have, unless they stand on this sure foundation of *unquestioned* and *unquestionable truth*, they must be kept out of our work here; for if the premises be faulty, or the relation sought to be traced only an imaginary one, the conclusions to be derived therefrom must inevitably be false, and very injurious to the pupil, since being received as truth, they prevent any further investigation of the subject on his part, and effectually bar his mind against the entrance of the truth if presented by others. For

Instance, the teacher who, in the study of the globe, directs the pupil's attention to the parallelism of the Atlantic coast, and leads him thence to the conclusion that the two worlds were once united and have been rent asunder, leaving this chasm between them, is guilty of a great wrong and injustice to the pupil. He has given him, instead of the truth, a falsehood, which, having arrived at it by what he believes to be a reasonable conclusion, he will hold, as he would hold the truth, with all the tenacity of conviction; and his ever arriving at the true solution of the question is a very doubtful matter. The judicious teacher will direct his attention to this parallelism as an interesting fact to be noticed and remembered, but will go no further. The cause of it (for it is not an accident) is entirely beyond his reach, and can only become accessible to him when, in his matured power, he shall be able to study the laws which operated to give the earth's surface its present conformation.

We proceed, then, with the distribution of the internal waters, and their arrangement into natural systems. A conversation like the following, between teacher and pupils, will lead to the tracing of these systems: "What and where is the largest river of North America?" "The Mississippi. Its source is in the height of land in the middle of the Great Central Plain, and it flows directly south into the Gulf of Mexico." "Where do all its greatest tributaries rise?" "Those from the west, in the Rocky Mountains; and those from the east, in the Appalachian system." "What did we learn about that part of the great plain along which the Mississippi flows?" "It is the lowest part of the plain, where the two slopes which form it meet." "In what direction do the tributaries from the Rocky Mountains flow?" "They flow eastward; those from the Appalachians, westward." "Why do not those from the Rocky Mountains continue to flow eastward, and those from the Appalachians to flow westward, instead of all uniting along this particular line to form the Mississippi?" "Each set flowed in their own direction until they reached the bottom of the slope down which they had started. Neither could go beyond the place in which the Mississippi is formed, because, in that case, they must flow *up hill*. They must either stop there, or turn and flow together along the bottom of their slopes." "Why did they not turn northward instead of southward?" "Because the middle part of the great plain is higher than the southern part, and the waters must always flow down the slope of land instead of up." The pupils thus are led to see that with the present form of that portion of the continent any other arrangement of its waters is impossible. The Mississippi occupies the place it does, not because "it happens to be there," but because *it cannot be anywhere else* while the continent continues in its present conformation. Let some one indicate the entire region which sends its waters to the Mississippi. We now give the name *river basin* to this region, and *river system* to all its lakes and rivers taken together. Proceeding in the same manner, we distinguish the other three great river basins and systems in the Central Plain—the St. Lawrence, the Hudson Bay, and the Mackenzie systems. We notice the fact that all these waters, coming principally from the Rocky- Mountains, find their way eventually to the Atlantic and Arctic Oceans.

We now seek the sources of the Pacific rivers. The children notice that all the greater streams also flow from the Rocky Mountains. Direct their attention to Union Peak, where, separated only by the breadth of the mountain, are, on one side, the sources of the Missouri; and, on the other, those of the Columbia and Colorado. One goes away thousands of miles eastward to the Atlantic, the others westward into the Pacific. Follow the mountain-range northward to Mount Brown, and we still find the same division of the waters. All the sources on the east slope send their waters eastward to the Atlantic and Arctic, while those on the west slope go westward to the Pacific. Can any one think why this should be so? A simple allusion to the two sloping parts of a roof, with the dividing ridge between them, will give the pupils the idea. This is the dividing ridge of the continent, the line of highest land, from which its two great slopes go away to the oceans bordering it; the longer to the Atlantic, the shorter to the Pacific. The Atlantic highland, as appears so distinctly upon the profile, is only a little swell, breaking this long slope.

The children will now comprehend why-we have those mighty rivers going from the country at the foot of the Rocky Mountains far away to the eastern ocean, thus giving access from the Atlantic to the whole great interior of the continent. Let them for a moment suppose that the Pacific and the Atlantic highlands have changed places, so that this great water-shed takes the place of the Appalachian Mountains, and-judge what must be the result on the distribution of the waters of the continent. All the great streams must go to the Pacific, and the Atlantic would receive none greater than those which have their source in the Appalachian Mountains.

. They will thus have taken their first step toward the future realization of the great fact, that the structure of this continent *is in no wise an accident*, but that it was made as it is by the Creator for a special purpose. When would Christian civilization have possessed this entire continent as it now does, if, in addition to the hostility of the indigenous race, it had been shut out from the fertile interior by the almost impassable barrier of the Rocky Mountains with the desert wastes on each side of them?

CLIMATE.—We have now finished the consideration of those topics which belong especially to the perceptive phase of the subject, and which must always constitute the main-work of pupils at this stage of their development. The remaining topics are added only in their most general facts, in order to give the pupil correct habits of regarding them, and thus prepare him for their extended and minute study in the succeeding grades; and also to give a simple exercise to the powers of mind most to be employed in that study,—the reasoning powers, which are now coming into action.

In order to introduce this topic, there must be a preparatory conversational exercise, in which the pupil becomes acquainted with the ideas expressed by the term climate, and the terms connected with it; as, a temperate climate, a moist climate, etc.; and with the fact that water is changed to vapor on being warmed; that the vapor returns to water on being cooled; that the ocean is the great source of the moisture spread over the lands; and that this moisture is carried from place to place by the winds. All these points can be made perfectly clear to him by means of illustrations drawn from simple phenomena of which he is every day a witness. The reasoning processes performed in the investigation of this point are a little more difficult to the pupil than in the preceding, because the premises from which they proceed are of a less tangible character, and cannot be so easily presented to his perception. Still, as we are aware, they can only be of the simplest character. It would, of course, be utterly impossible for the child of ten years to go through all the processes of reasoning by which we arrive at a knowledge of the causes of the climatic conditions peculiar to different parts of North America. Nor is this at all necessary, either to give an intelligent and lasting knowledge of such of those conditions as are important for him to know, or to afford his reasoning power a just amount of exercise. Every extended course of reasoning involves many successive conclusions, which in their turn become the data from which we proceed to draw other conclusions. Ascending the chain in search of causes, we inevitably arrive at some data beyond which, even in our highest development, we have no power to go—some fact or condition to which we can assign no cause, other than the will of God that it should exist, and which must therefore be accepted as the starting point for all our reasoning. Descending in search of results, the same inevitable limit finally meets us. The *ultimate*, *either in cause or consequence*, is unattainable to human reason. The child may do with his limited power precisely what we can do with our greater power. He may begin from the most remote cause attainable by *his* powers of reasoning, and proceed to the most distant result they are capable of reaching, and derive the same benefit and satisfaction from his limited exercise which we derive from our more extended one. We may give him any one of the successive results attained in our process of reasoning, to be the beginning of his, *provided only* that he is capable of taking *with ease* the next step in advance.

For instance, we cannot make the child comprehend the causes of a regular diminution of heat from the equator toward the poles; neither can he comprehend the cause of the existence, in the tropical regions, of the invariable trade-winds, nor the prevalence, in the extra tropical, of the return trades. For the present, he must content himself with the knowledge that these things exist; but if he is able readily to trace, by the exercise of his reasoning powers, even but one of the effects produced by the existence of these things (and he can trace more than one), it is his right to be permitted and aided to do so, instead of being obliged to accept and remember them, on the authority of others, without the aid of his own intelligence. Suppose it is required that the pupil shall learn a description of the climate, vegetation, and animal life of the continent, such as is usually given in common school geographies, of which the following is a brief summary:

The main body of the Continent of North America, that lying between Hudson's Bay and the Gulf of Mexico, has a temperate climate, with long winters in the north and long summers in the south.

The small northern part of the continent is exceedingly cold, almost a constant winter; while the south is exceedingly warm, a constant summer throughout the year.

The different portions of the great temperate region differ remarkably in regard to moisture. The Central Plain and the Atlantic highlands have, in general, abundant rains throughout the year; while, on the Pacific highland, rain rarely falls except upon the mountains. The narrow coast region west of the Sierra Nevada also has abundant rains. The climate is in general remarkably healthful.

The tropical regions in the south have daily violent rains during one-half the year, which is therefore called the wet season. The remainder of the year is almost destitute of rain, and is called the dry season. The climate is in general very unhealthful, except in the highlands of the interior, where the air is cooler and drier.

* "The regions bordering the Arctic Ocean are among the most dreary on the face of the earth. The shores are covered with eternal snows, and the entire surface of the sea with large fields and huge masses of floating ice. There is scarcely any vegetation in the north capable of supporting the existence of man. An abundance of mosses, lichens, berries, willows, and shrubs grow, upon which birds and land animals subsist. These frozen regions, though thinly peopled,

* The portions quoted are from one of the best Common School Geographies now in use.

abound with animal life both upon land and in the sea. The lakes abound with fish, and myriads of waterfowl hover upon the coast. The principal amphibious animals are the seal and walrus. The white bear inhabits the northern coasts, reindeer are numerous, and immense numbers of the smaller fur-bearing animals are yearly taken by trappers.

"The temperate region differs greatly in different parts in regard to vegetation and animals. The region between the Sierra Nevada and Rocky Mountains is generally barren. Most of the country west of the Sierra Nevada is exceedingly fertile, and capable of supporting a dense population. The Coast range of mountains is covered with vegetation to its summit. A desert plateau extends along the base of the Rocky Mountains, stretching eastward to a distance of two hundred or four hundred miles.

"The soil of the central plain is generally very rich. Most of the States of Wisconsin and Illinois, and much of the country west of the Mississippi River, consist of prairie land. The prairies are not, however, entirely destitute of timber, but are well wooded near the banks of the streams. The land is fertile and yields a natural growth of heavy grass. The St. Lawrence Basin is a well-wooded, fertile region. The Alleghany Mountains are covered with vegetation to their summits. The various grains are raised in all parts of the country. The potato succeeds best in the Northern States. Its place is supplied in the South by the sweet potato. Hemp and flax thrive in the middle districts," and "tobacco is principally raised in the middle sections. Most of the cotton used by mankind is raised in the Southern States. Rice grows abundantly in the South in marshy tracts along the coast. In the extreme South, sugar is one of the most important productions, and oranges are easily raised."

At the discovery of the country the whole region east of the Mississippi was covered with dense forests, in which were found multitudes of deers, bears, wolves, wild cats, and other animals. On the prairies of the Mississippi were great herds of bisons. These animals have now nearly disappeared, having been driven away by the settlement of the country.

The grizzly bear, panther, and other wild animals are very numerous in the few forests of the Pacific highlands. The tropical regions of the South have in general a most abundant and luxuriant vegetation. Instead of the pine, oak, maple, and walnut, the forests are filled with the palm, mahogany, and rosewood, and a great variety of other trees that grow only in warm countries. The rivers and marshes are filled with alligators, turtles, and other reptiles, and the air swarms with a multitude of insects of every variety, some of them very dangerous. On the table lands of Mexico the forests and animals are like those of the temperate and the cold regions of the continent.

Ordinary pupils would require a vast amount of study to commit this to memory, and make a good recitation upon it; and in the majority of cases if, after a week had passed, one were to be examined upon it without the opportunity to study it anew, he would not be able to give even a tolerable description of any one of these different portions of the continent. The moist regions and the dry, the barren regions and the fruitful, would be mingled together in his mind in hopeless confusion. Now there is hardly one of the foregoing catalogue of facts, except the tropical rains, and the enumeration of particular kinds of plants and animals found in any given region, which he cannot perfectly well ascertain for himself by a very simple process of thought (it can hardly be called reasoning), having as a starting point *the structure of the continent*, which he knows thoroughly, and these two fundamental facts—the decreasing temperature from the equator toward the poles, and the prevalence in the temperate portion of the continent of southwest winds. Many steps of the investigation will be only the presentation of an analogy to some simple phenomenon with which every child is perfectly familiar. When this investigation is finished, he will have all these important facts grouped together in the order of their dependence; and so identified with the structure of the continent that it will be impossible for him to forget or to confuse them, without obliterating the map from his memory, which, after having studied it in the manner indicated, *can never be done*, any more than you can strike out from his recollection the image of the house dog or the cat with which he daily plays.

The most fundamental of climatic conditions is that of temperature, and this is therefore to be first ascertained. For this the pupil needs only to examine the globe, bearing in mind that the warmest parts of the earth are those about the equator, the coldest parts about the poles, while the regions midway are temperate.

We now study the temperate portion of the continent in reference to moisture. We recall the ideas previously presented, that the ocean is the great source of the moisture distributed over the land; that the winds are the carriers of this moisture; that as vapor rises more abundantly from warm than from cold water, the winds that blow upon a country from warm oceans will be the ones to bring it

3

most moisture. The teacher, placing the map before the pupils asks which are the warmest waters bordering the main body of the continent, and in what direction they are from it. "The Gulf on the south, and the Pacific on the southwest." "What winds, then, will bring moist moisture to this part of the continent?" "Those from the south and southwest." He now tells them of the south and southwest winds constantly blowing across this part of the continent from the Gulf and the warm part of the Pacific; and asks some one to show the part of the continent over which the Gulf winds would sweep. (A line drawn from the western shore of the Gulf directly north, would cut off to the east all that part of the continent which is reached by the south winds; while a line from the same point parallel with the Atlantic coast, gives the sweep of the southwest winds.) "Since those winds carry such quantities of vapor from the warm waters of the Gulf, what may we judge to be the case in regard to the amount of moisture falling on this eastern part of the continent?" "There will probably be a great abundance of moisture in all parts of the year." He now tells the pupils of the great amount of moisture which this region receives, and of the fact that, though the Atlantic furnishes a small portion, it is nearly all derived from the Gulf.

He now directs their attention to the western half of the temperate region (the part lying in the United States), which is beyond the reach of the Gulf winds. "Whence are these Pacific highlands to obtain moisture?" "From the Pacific Ocean." "What forms the western border of the Pacific highlands?" (referring to profile). "The high mountain wall of the Sierra Nevada." "What do you remember about these mountains?" "They are so high that their tops are constantly covered with snow and ice." "If that is the case, then all this upper portion must be very cold. Has any one ever seen a cold plate placed where the steam from warm water could strike it?" Many have seen this. "What happens to the plate?" "It becomes covered with drops of water." "Where does the water come from?" "The steam changes to water when it is cooled by the plate." "Now these warm winds, full of vapor from the the Pacific, come sweeping over the continent. They find in their pathway the high cold wall of the Sierra Nevada, which they must climb and cross. What will happen to the vapor when it comes near this cold wall?" "Much of it will be changed to water, and fall in rain, and the wind will go over the mountains without it." "What difference between the wind after it has crossed the mountains, and before it reached them?" "It was warm and moist, now it is much colder and drier." "When this wind from the mountains is crossing the table lands, which are lower and warmer than they, will it become warmer or cooler?" "Warmer." "If, then, the table lands warm the wind instead of cooling it, can the wind give them rain?" "It cannot, because the vapor must be cooled before it will fall in rain." "When this wind which has become warm in crossing the table land, reaches the Rocky Mountains, which are even higher and colder than the Sierra Nevada, what will happen?" "It will be cooled again, and the moisture which the Sierra Nevada left remaining in it, will fall in rain on the Rocky Mountains." "What will be the condition in regard to moisture of the table land at the east of the Rocky Mountains?" "That also will be without rain, for the ocean wind has become perfectly dry, and we shall find no more rain until we reach the country swept by the Gulf winds." The teacher tells the pupils now that their conclusions are very correct; that the coast regions west of the mountain border of the table land have abundant rains, but that the whole great highland region in this portion of the continent has very little rain except among the mountains.

VEGETATION AND ANIMALS.—The teacher now appeals to the pupil's experience in gardening, and elicits the facts that plants cannot grow without both warmth and moisture. He then says: "We find that this great temperate region of the continent, though much alike in its different parts, in regard to warmth, is very unlike in regard to moisture. The eastern half has everywhere a great abundance of rain, while the western half, except on the Pacific coast and among the mountains, is almost destitute of rain. "What difference may we expect to find in these two regions in regard to plants?" "We may expect an abundant vegetation in all parts of the eastern; while, in the western, there will be very little vegetation except upon the mountains, and beyond the Sierra Nevada." Their conclusion in this respect will now be confirmed by a description of the luxuriant forests that covered the entire East on the discovery of the country; the wealth of vegetation of the Pacific coast regions, and the almost complete absence of it on the great interior table lands, except in the region of the mountains. Recalling the fact that the East owes its moisture to the Gulf of Mexico, ask them to suppose that there "had not happened to be" a great arm of the sea thrust thus into the heart of the continent, and imagine the results upon that, the richest and most fruitful part of America. They will thus have made another step towards the comprehension of the fact that there is a purpose in the structure of the continent.

A similar plan will lead to an understanding of the absence of vegetation in the cold region, and the great wealth of it in the Tropical portion of the continent. After this the distribution of animals is perfectly comprehensible, not at all as a consequence of the vegetable life, but simply as in association with it. Where there is abundant sustenance for animal life, we may naturally expect to find animals numerous, and *vice versâ*.

The pupils now have a correct, thorough, and intelligent knowledge of all that appertains to the general physical conditions of the continent. They are, therefore, prepared to gain easily and with pleasure, a thorough and intelligent knowledge of all that belongs to the general social condition and industries of its inhabitants. Without this preparation the latter would have been wholly unintelligible to them, would have been learned with difficulty, and quickly forgotten.

We have seen how almost entirely this study of the continent is confined to the examination of the map, and we thus see how absolutely indispensable is a *correct physical* map. Having this, the

particular text-book which the pupil may use is of little consequence, for the map is the subject of study, and the principal use
of the book is to give him a convenient summary of what he has
already read upon the map. Of course, that book which repro-
duces most nearly in a concise manner what is figured upon the
map, with a few of the most important additional details, is the
most desirable one. Still, as we must acknowledge, the pupil may,
under the guidance of a judicious teacher, dispense with any other
book than that which he could make for himself by writing out
each day what he has read upon the map, and adding to it such
details as any intelligent teacher would give in connection with it.

STATES AND NATIONS.—We enter now on an entirely different
field of study. Heretofore we have been studying the continent as
it came perfected from the hand of the Creator. Now we study it
as occupied by, and under the control of man, for whose abode it
was constructed.

In studying the eighth point, the *races* which inhabit the continent, the pupil has nothing to do but to remember what is told
him. He has no means of ascertaining for himself any thing about
them. But in this last point, the people in their social capacity of
states and nations, he can again do very much by the proper exercise of his own powers of mind.

Preparatory to this, there must be a series of conversational exercises in which the pupil's own nature is brought to his conscious-
ness. He finds himself to have a threefold existence, body, mind,
and soul, each having wants peculiar to itself—the body of food,
clothing, and shelter—the mind of guidance and instruction in all
truths attainable by the intelligence of man—and the soul of instruction in regard to its origin, duties, and destiny.

He learns of the classification of mankind as civilized or
savage, according to the degree to which these wants are realized,
and the manner in which, and extent to which, they are supplied.
Finally, he learns of the great resources of civilized nations in
providing means for the supply of these wants—agriculture and

grazing, lumbering, mining, manufacturing, and commerce ;—which of these are most feasible in any given physical conditions which a country may possess ;—and which are the most desirable locations for any particular occupation, as manufacturing or commerce, and which require the assemblage of large communities in limited areas, and thus give rise to towns and cities.

Now the pupil is ready to return to the map. The territory occupied by any nation in a continent being defined, by tracing its boundaries upon the physical map, he, knowing all the general physical conditions of that country, knows at once what are the resources of the people inhabiting it ; what it is capable of being in the hands of an intelligent and industrious community. He knows where are the best facilities for agriculture—where pasturage would be more practicable—where are the regions of forests and mines—where are the best locations for manufacturing and commerce ; and, hence, where he may expect to find thriving towns. In looking at the physical map, therefore, he sees, in imagination, a busy people carrying on in every part of the country the appropriate avocations. If he finds that these resources are not improved as they are capable of being, he argues a limited population or an imperfect civilization.

If, on the contrary, he turns to his text-book and reads, in reference to the United States, of the concentration of almost the entire population in the eastern half of the country,—the great manufacturing, mining, and commercial enterprise of the Northeast—the devotion of the mass of people to agriculture in the South and the Central Plain—the exclusive mining in the Western highlands—the commercial importance of New York, New Orleans, San Francisco, and Chicago—he finds nothing that is strange, uninteresting, or difficult to remember. He understands it all, for he possesses the one only key which unlocks the mystery of the topography and resources of states and nations, that is the *physical conformation and condition* of the country they occupy.

The history of their growth as a nation is also made intelligible by the same means. No one who has attentively studied the history

of the early settlement of North America, and the growth of our
country to its present dimensions, can have failed to remark the
important influence which the peculiar conformation of the continent has had upon it.

The Spaniards, attracted by the mineral wealth of the mountains, established themselves in Central America and Mexico, and
eventually appropriated Florida. The French, obtaining possession
of the mouths of the St. Lawrence and the Mississippi, these great
arteries of the continent, claimed the entire interior accessible by
them. Thus every part of the continent accessible to Europe, ex
cept the narrow band east of the Appalachian Mountains, was already appropriated when the English Puritans, impelled not by love
of gain or desire for territory, but driven " for conscience' sake"
to abandon their country, sought a home among its rugged hills.
Accessions to their numbers constantly arrived, and they spread
themselves, undisputed except by the indigenous race, until they
occupied the entire band east of the mountains. Now they began
to extend themselves westward across this barrier, by means of
the natural passage opened through the valley of the Hudson and
Mohawk. The moment that step was taken, they encountered a
stronger foe. The French claimed the interior, and the French
and Indian War was only a mode of solving the great question—
were the English to be permitted to pass this natural barrier?
That question settled in their favor, a grand future opened before
the English colonies. They saw themselves already the possessors
of this great continent; and feeling the control which the home
government exercised over them, an obstacle to their advancement
in the path marked out for them by Providence, they resolved to
rid themselves of it, and this resolution was followed by another
struggle, and the solving of another question. The possessor of
this goodly heritage was not to be one of the old monarchies of
Europe.

Now an unimpeded progress began across the great interior
plains. Possessing themselves, by purchase and treaty, of these
lands as fast as they were able to occupy them, the new nation soon

reached the second great barrier, the Rocky Mountains. Here another foe met them. The Spaniards, intrenched in the rich mining country beyond, disputed their passage. Another war solved another question. The " westward march of empire" should find no limit but the sea.

Thus we see how intimately every important matter connected with the nations which occupy a country, is blended with its physical conformation; and thus we see, as before stated, the necessity of a thorough knowledge of the latter, in order to pursue the intelligent study of the former.

When the general course here indicated has been pursued in each of the six continents, and a general view is had of the conformation of the oceans, the main work of the *perceptive* course is done. The pupil is now thoroughly prepared to enter upon the *analytic* course, in which he is no longer confined mainly to the study of general forms, but the detailed modifications of these forms are carefully considered. A great store of facts is acquired in regard to the life of the vegetation, animals, man, and nations associated with them, and the pupil is constantly employing his reasoning powers in tracing the relation of these facts to the physical conditions with which they are associated.

We are aware that the ideas here advanced are diametrically opposed to the generally received notions in regard to the proper presentation of this subject to the young; and that if acted upon, they must produce an entire revolution in our methods of teaching Geography.

We trust it has been made evident to the reader that, if we are to proceed on philosophic principles, the old plan of giving the pupil long lists of names, and collections of facts in regard to political geography, as his first work in this subject, must be set aside; and he must, in the outset, be introduced to the globe in its physical conformation and conditions.

Years of experience have convinced the writer that if the general plan here indicated be pursued, we shall no longer hear the complaint, so often made by teachers, that the children do not learn their geography lessons; are not interested in them, and do not remember them.

The text-book so often disliked and neglected by the pupil, will become (if properly arranged) but the summary of his own thoughts, a convenient memorandum of facts and relations, most of which he has himself discovered, to which he will always turn with interest and pleasure. The few details given in regard to such points as are beyond the range of his investigation, in their relation to such points as he has investigated, will confirm the justness of his own conclusions, and will therefore be perused with never-wearying delight.

NOTE.—The general principles here discussed, and the plan presented for the treatment of the subject of Geography with the young, are those exemplified in the first two books of "Guyot's Geographical Series." The "Primary" book is intended to cover the ground indicated as a *preparatory course*, while the "Common School Geography" is the pupil's manual in the perceptive course proper, the "*Study of the Globe and Maps.*" It is a memorandum of facts to be learned by this study, with such additional details and exercises as are important to the pupil of twelve or thirteen years, the age at which this course is supposed to be completed.

3*

A KEY

FOR THE

USE OF GUYOT'S WALL ATLAS.

PART I.

THE USE OF A MAP IN TEACHING GEOGRAPHY.

L.—*Necessity of Maps as a means of Geographical Study.*

THOUGH we are far from the time in which many attempted to teach geography without the aid of maps, it still may be said that not sufficient use is made of them. Rather should we perhaps say, the use which is made of them is not the proper one—not that which is indispensable to successful teaching.

The principal geographical element is the relative situation of physical objects, and of countries, cities, &c. Nothing can adequately convey this to the mind of the young except the sight of the objects themselves, placed in their true position.

The study of any natural object, as a flower, or an animal, cannot be rightly conducted unless the object itself is presented, examined, and analyzed, until its form is so impressed upon the mind of the pupil as to remain at all times present to his imagination.

The study of the earth, as a physical object, would require a similar method; but the earth is too large an object to be taken hold of in this manner. The keenest eye, from the summit of the highest mountain upon the globe, can perceive but a very small portion of its surface; and cannot at all ascertain its form. Supposing even that the beholder could be raised much higher still, so that his view should embrace one hemisphere, yet would the other remain

3*

unseen by him. Nor would the portion of the globe thus seen have sufficient distinctness to convey any adequate idea of the true nature of its surface.

We must, therefore, resort to other means in the study of the earth. A representation of the globe on a smaller scale, more adapted to our powers of vision, is the only possible means of supplying this need. The artificial globe, presenting the great outlines of the continents, oceans, streams, and mountains, in their true relative situation, must become the object of study instead of the real globe. But a globe, even if it be of considerable size, will scarcely allow sufficient details for the purposes of geographical teaching. Besides this, the globe presents to the eye only one-half of the earth's surface at a time, which prevents a general study of the relative sizes and situations of the continents, and the comparison of their forms. The simultaneous view of all the continents, which is necessary to the study of their relations to each other and to the oceans, is a desideratum which the globe cannot afford.

We are obliged, therefore, to resort to simple map representations, upon flat surfaces, with the unavoidable difficulty and inconvenience of that distortion which results from this representation of a curved surface upon a flat surface.

To study a physical map of the globe and of each continent, each having in itself all of the most prominent and characteristic features of every land, must and should be the first, nay, nearly the sole object of elementary teaching in geography. Says the great reformer of geographical study, Carl Ritter: "Let the pupil have a box before you, require him to put any thing into it; then what you give him will be permanently retained." Such a box is a good fundamental *physical map* of the globe and of each country. Having this fixed in his mind, let the pupil read books of travel or of history, descriptions of people, or of plants or animals, and he will at once locate every geographical detail in its proper place, and will surely remember what he reads all the better; while at the same time he is constantly perfecting the image in his own mind of the real nature of the continent, of the country he reads about, as it actually is. Without this foundation, it is idle to begin to study geography; for no one of those acts which geography, civil and physical, undertakes to teach, will be in its proper place, and consequently it can neither be under stood nor remembered.

II.—*The requisites of a School Map.*

It is a great error, productive of much mischief, to suppose that almost any map, however rough and incorrect, is good enough for the beginner, and for the walls of the schoolroom. From the nature of the mind, the first impressions received, especially in childhood, are the most lasting. The image of the first map which the child has seen and studied, is likely to remain in his mind and accompany him through life. If this first image is incorrect, instead of being a help, it is a serious drawback in all his subsequent studies. The school map is the foundation of his geographical knowledge, and should be true, solid, and correct, if the superstructure is to be so.

The essential qualities of a good school map, we conceive to be the following:

First.—IT SHOULD BE CORRECT; however few are the geographical features that it admits, they should be true to nature, and should give the most reliable representation that can be obtained of the portion of the globe which the map is designed to illustrate.

Second.—CLEARNESS AND SIMPLICITY are important requisites. " *Only the maps which look empty are well remembered,*" says Humboldt. Only such features of the coasts, mountains, rivers, cities, &c., as are to be remembered as fundamental and characteristic, are to be admitted; and those less important, which would complicate and obscure the map, should be omitted. Such a selection is not easy, since it requires the science and judgment of a master of the subject, as well as the experience of a reflecting teacher.

Third.—THE PRE-EMINENT IMPORTANCE OF THE PHYSICAL FEATURES, that is, of the permanent groundwork of nature, over the statistical details of cities, states, boundaries, &c., or the transient work of man, should be recognized, and regulate and govern the mode of representation. The most salient outlines of the vertical configuration, therefore, or of the surface relief—the peculiar and varied forms of which so strikingly distinguish each of the great continents from all the others—should be carefully but boldly expressed by a suitable method of drawing, and by numerous profiles. For it must be remembered that the very nature of a country, its climatic divisions, its drainage and river systems, its productions and economic value, the civil and political conditions of its inhabitants, are most intimately connected with those forms of elevation and depression which constitute its lowlands, plateaus, and mountainous regions. To neglect this all-important element, is to deprive the map of its chief usefulness; and yet it is well known that the school maps now in use are most deficient in this respect.

Fourth.—HARMONY, or the expression of the true relative proportions of parts as found in nature, is another essential quality. The prominence or subordination of each physical feature in the map should conform to its prominence or subordination in nature. The Appalachian system in North America, with its crests of 3,000 feet, and its highest peaks of 6,000 feet, should not appear as prominent as the Rocky Mountains and the Sierra Nevada, with their broad base of 6,000 feet of elevation, and their summits of 12,000 to 15,000 feet. Nor should the third-rank table-land and mountains of Brazil, of 2,500 and 7,000 feet altitude, appear to rival in importance the lofty plateaus of the Andes, which, by their mass, their elevation of 12,000 to 14,000 feet, and the gigantic peaks of 20,000 to 25,000 feet, borne on their broad shoulders, are in the first rank among the grand geographical forms of our planet. Wherever that natural gradation of the leading physical features is wanting, the map loses its power of expressing the real nature of the relief, as well as the true relation of its parts, and totally fails to convey to the pupil the idea of the natural structure of the continent.

III.—*Guyot's Wall Atlas.*

These series of wall maps have been prepared in accordance with the views expressed above, and possess, it is hoped, all the characteristics there mentioned.

More than usual care has been bestowed on the illustration of that most important, though much-neglected geographical element, *the forms of relief,* or the elevations and depressions of the surface. The differences of altitudes of lowlands and plateaus, which cannot well be rendered by any mode of topographical drawing, are expressed by different tints; while in the various mountain chains the boldness of the topographical drawing increases with their elevation and importance; thus establishing, in the mind of the pupil, their relative gradation, and the true proportions which exist in nature. With these aids, and the numerous profiles which are found in each map, it becomes an easy task for the instructor to teach, and for the pupil to understand and remember, these fundamental features of the structure of each continent; and to recognize, by the comparison of the differences so strongly marked in the map, the special character and individual type presented by each of our great masses of land.

It will be remarked, on an examination of the maps of the several continents, that while green is the color chosen to represent the lowlands, the number of feet of altitude covered by the green, and therefore characterized as low land, is not the same in all the maps. Thus the green in North America represents an average elevation of surface below 800 feet; in Europe below 600 feet; in Asia below 1,000 feet. This may appear calculated to create confusion in the mind of both teacher and pupil. It should, however, be remembered that the expressions *lowland* and *highland* are not absolute, but relative. In indicating them we can adopt no uniform standard for all the continents, any more than we can insist upon a uniform length of the arm for all men. That which would be a *long* arm for one man, would be a disproportionately *short* arm for a man of higher stature. So, in indicating the surface of the continents, we must have reference in each to the individual scale upon which the continent is constructed. That which would be *high* land in Europe, the general elevation of which is so little above the level of the sea (see profile, "The Old World from East to West," upon the Map of the World), would be *low land* in Asia, the average elevation of which is nearly double that of Europe. A uniform standard, therefore, would fail to express in either one or the other maps the very relations of internal structure which it is designed to illustrate.

In the Map of the World, where the continents are to be compared with each other in regard to elevation, all are colored according to the same scale. In the maps of the individual continents, however, the object is not to show the absolute elevation of surface in all parts of the earth; but to show, what is of vastly greater importance to the pupil, the relative average elevation of different portions of the same continent. Therefore, each is colored according to its own individual scale, without reference to any other.

In addition to the preceding features, the nature of the surface, whether forest land, prairie, or deserts, will be found indicated by special signs, where these phenomena are sufficiently characteristic to be thus noted; and also the limits of the zones of the vegetable staples which distinguish the great divisions of climate; together with the marine currents which sweep along the coasts.

But while the maps are thus essentially physical, the political boundaries of states being marked, and the principal cities lettered on the maps, they can be used, when desired, as political maps, and then possess the great advantage of showing, at the same time, the often very dissimilar nature and capacities of the various countries or parts of one country which are united under the same political rule.

A last feature of the maps, which, we doubt not, will be much appreciated by teachers, is that, while practically they are mute for the pupil, they are not so for the instructor. Absolutely mute maps are very often illegible. It is not always easy, even for a practised and well-informed teacher, to fasten, immediately, the right name on a second and third rank river, mountain, or city, marked on the maps. Even initials, as found on some wall maps, will not entirely obviate the difficulty. In the maps we are considering all the principal mountains, rivers, and cities are given in full, in clear type, but small enough to prevent their being read from the position occupied by the reciting pupil. The teacher, moreover, will find in each map a vast amount of information, including, besides names, heights of mountains and of table-lands which will save him much time and labor.

IV.—Map Drawing.

In our general discussion on the method of studying the map of North America (see *Geographical Teaching*, pages 29 to 55 inclusive), we have indicated the plan which should be carried out in the study of all maps of the continents, or of portions of the continents, as the maps of the *United States* and *Central Europe*. We have endeavored to show that when the pupil once knows how to read the maps, he has but to apply to it his own powers of observation and thought, and he will derive from it all that is most important for him to know in regard to the physical conformation and character of the region which it represents, and its capabilities in the hands of a civilized people.

A test must, however, be applied, in order that the teacher may ascertain whether the pupil has in his imagination a correct picture of the country, as shown upon the map. Such a test is afforded by map drawing *from memory*, which should be required of the pupil.

We have also, in our study of North America, insisted upon map drawing as the most effectual means of imprinting upon the memory the characteristic features of the continent. Mere copying the map, though better than no drawing at all, is not sufficient, either as a means of study, or to test the thoroughness and accuracy of the pupil's knowledge of the country under consideration. Many a pupil who has copied the map of a continent successfully and repeatedly, will yet have no accurate knowledge of the relative position of prominent points upon it, nor of the direction and comparative extent of different portions of its contour and area, all of which are essential to a correct idea of its form. Much less will he have any accurate conception of the relative position of the different continents upon the globe, which is essential to the comprehension of their relations one to another. To secure the needed accuracy in a knowledge of these things, the pupil should construct maps of the continents, in some manner which will compel him to study carefully the general form and the internal arrangement of each; after which he should construct a map of the world in a manner which will require him to remark carefully the position of each continent upon the globe.

We give diagrams for the construction of a map of each continent, by means of which this close study of its form is secured; and by means of which even the pupil having the very least facility in using his pencil, who would never be able to draw any thing correctly by mere copying, can yet make an accurate map. The teacher is supposed to draw, in the presence of the class, the several portions of the diagram, in the order indicated in the "directions" which accompany each. Before drawing each line, he repeats to the pupils the "direction" for drawing it when the line drawn by him serves as a guide to them in obeying his instructions.* A few lessons will fix this diagram in the memory of every pupil, after which he cannot fail always to produce a correct map. The degree of elegance attained by each will of course depend upon the taste and skill of each pupil; but the work of all will be equally accurate, provided the several directions are obeyed with exactness. The three southern continents, it will be remarked, have a much more simple structure than the northern. It would, therefore, be well that the pupils begin with those, leaving the northern continents for a later period, when the practice upon the southern shall have given them a degree of facility in drawing lines of any given length in any given direction.

In employing the "Map-Drawing Cards" upon which the parallels and meridians are traced, the "lines of construction" may be dispensed with. The pupil then has but to commit to memory the latitude and longitude of the points or *angles* of the *fundamental form* (three in each, North America, South America, Africa, and Europe, four in Asia, and five in Australia). He then places these points upon the proper card in the given latitude and longitude, and connects them by straight lines. Thus is the fundamental form at once secured.

The construction lines are, however, indispensable in drawing, except upon map-drawing cards. They afford the only means of invariably placing upon the slate, or blackboard, the different points of the fundamental, or of the approximate form, in their correct relative position. When the fundamental form is once obtained, the drawing is completed in a uniform manner, whether upon the cards, or upon the slate, or the blackboard.

Having the latitude and longitude of the different angles of the fundamental form of each continent, and knowing how to draw each

* For additional details in regard to this exercise, see *Teacher's Edition* of *Common School Geography.*

correctly, the pupil can now combine them all into a correct Map of the World.

From the diagrams it is apparent that, by simple divisions of the main lines of the continent, the approximate location of almost every important point on its contour can be obtained. The same method, as is seen by the "internal construction" of North America, may also be applied to the location of its principal mountain and river systems.

Having been taught to draw the maps in this manner, the pupil will be able to draw either a map of a continent, or of the world, just as readily and accurately without a printed map before him as with one, and he will have secured a minuteness and accuracy of knowledge in regard to the form of the continents, the comparative size, and relative positions, of all the main features of its structure, which he could in no other way have obtained.

Such a study of every continent of our globe once completed, the pupil is ready for the study of every one of the various geographical or physical phenomena which shall in future present themselves for his consideration. He has acquired a precise and definite knowledge of geographical structure and location, without which all true geographical knowledge is well-nigh impossible.

V.—*Order of Geographical Study.*

With regard to the natural order in which the different classes of geographical facts or phenomena are to be presented in the study of the continents, it has already been shown that the particular class which is indispensable to the comprehension of the others, and which can be studied independently, must be presented first. The others follow successively in the order required by their natural connection, as cause and effect. A little additional discussion of this subject may, however, not be useless.

The configuration of the great land-masses—their form, their structure, their relief, the arrangement of their table-lands, mountain systems, and plains—can be studied irrespective of the system of water-courses, climate, productions, and the races of men which inhabit the continent. But the reverse is not true; for the river systems, their mode of combination, the direction in which they flow, the rapidity of their currents, all are entirely controlled by the elevations and depressions of the surface of the continent, and the arrangement of its mountain chains. It is obvious, therefore, that no intelligent study of the distribution of the falling waters, or the hydrography of the continent, is possible without reference to these forms of relief.

The general climate of the continent depends upon the general laws which govern the distribution of heat, the normal course of the winds, and the seasons of rain in various latitudes, which laws are more or less connected with the spherical form of the globe. These general climatic conditions are, however, greatly modified by the size of the continents, the relative amount of land and water that each contains, and still more by the elevation of the country above the level of the sea, and the situation and direction of mountain chains, including their particular position in reference to the prevailing winds which bring heat or cold, rain or drought.

The particular climate of any separate continent, or of any given region in that continent, can therefore be understood and fully described only when the entire physical configuration of the continent has been studied, and is viewed in connection with its position upon the globe.

The vast importance of the element of *altitude* in modifying the climate belonging to a given latitude, appears in its full force when we remember that a place whose elevation above the level of the sea exceeds that of another by only 300 or 350 feet, has an average temperature *one degree Fahrenheit lower* than that of the other place. The average elevation of that portion of Western New York which lies south of the parallel of the Mohawk River, is from 1,000 to 1,500 feet above the level of the sea. This gives it an average temperature similar to that of places which are at the level of the sea, some three or four hundred miles further north. The influence of such a decrease of temperature upon the capabilities of the country is obvious.

In higher systems of mountains, the natural contrasts caused by difference of elevation are still more striking. In the very heart of the tropical regions of South America, side by side with the burning plains of the Amazon, teeming with luxuriant vegetation, we behold the high, cold, and barren summits of the Andes, with their fields of eternal snow. The two are separated by only three miles of vertical distance, within which are found all the intermediate grades of temperature, and varying vegetation, which occur between the equator and the poles. In Asia, the burning plains of Hindostan are side by side and in nearly the same latitude with the giant peaks of the Himalayas, clothed with eternal snows from ten to fifteen thousand feet below their summits.

That powerful influence exerted by the altitude of a country upon its climate and its productions, acts with no less effect upon the amount of population, upon their habits, commerce, social conditions, and relations with other people. The structure of the Asiatic continent, and the modifications of its climate and fertility, arising from its varied forms of relief, can alone explain the wide difference which exists now, and has existed in all times, between the limited numbers and half-civilized condition of the nomadic tribes which roam over the dreary wastes of Mongolia, and the teeming millions, the civilization, and the abundant resources which are found in the low plains of China proper.

Much slighter differences in the physical character will, under other circumstances, have a most marked effect upon the character of the people of a country. In our own country, among the highest chains of the Appalachian mountain system, are the valleys of Eastern Tennessee and Western North Carolina, at an average elevation of 1,000 to 2,000 feet. This altitude, excluding the cultivation of cotton and making slavery unprofitable, left the people loyal to the old flag. Thus was found a little island of freedom and loyalty, in the midst of the surrounding ocean of slavery and secession.

The order, therefore, in which the different geographical topics are to be presented for study, is: First, the position, area, and contours of the continent, followed by its surface and relief. Next the system of drainage, or the inland waters, which are studied with constant reference to the relief of the surface. Next, are the phenomena of climate, connected with which are the vegetable and animal life of the continent; and last of all is its ethnological and political, or civil, geography, *the Geography of Man.*

It is obvious that if the pupil has been well trained, these various orders of facts will all be connected in his mind one with another; and the knowledge thus acquired will give him a sure and permanent foundation for the study of the subject, under its higher and properly scientific aspects.

We give, in Part II., a few of the leading facts to be derived from the study of each map in the series. The manner of presenting to the mind of the young these facts, namely, the physical structure of the continent and the relations of that structure to its entire character and capabilities, and to its political geography, has been illustrated in the "Study of the Map of North America," given in the preceding portion of this book, on *Geographical Teaching.* It rests with the individual teacher to judge, having reference to the age and advancement of his pupils, how much of the matter presented below should be given to them.

PART II.

STUDY OF THE MAPS.

NORTH AMERICA.

DIRECTIONS FOR THE CONSTRUCTION OF THE MAP.

1. CONSTRUCTION LINES.—1. Draw near the top of the slate the horizontal line A, the length desired for the width of the map.

2. From its middle draw the vertical line B, a little longer than A. Divide the right-hand half of A into three *equal* parts, *marking one of these parts M*, as it is an exact measure of many portions of the map. At the right-hand end of A, draw a second vertical line, O, making it a very little less than two M in length. These three lines are not parts of the map, but the ones on which the map is to be built, and may therefore be called *construction* lines. (Dotted on the model.)

GENERAL FORM.—1. Trace the line D between the lower end of O, and the left end of A, and we have the line of the north coast.

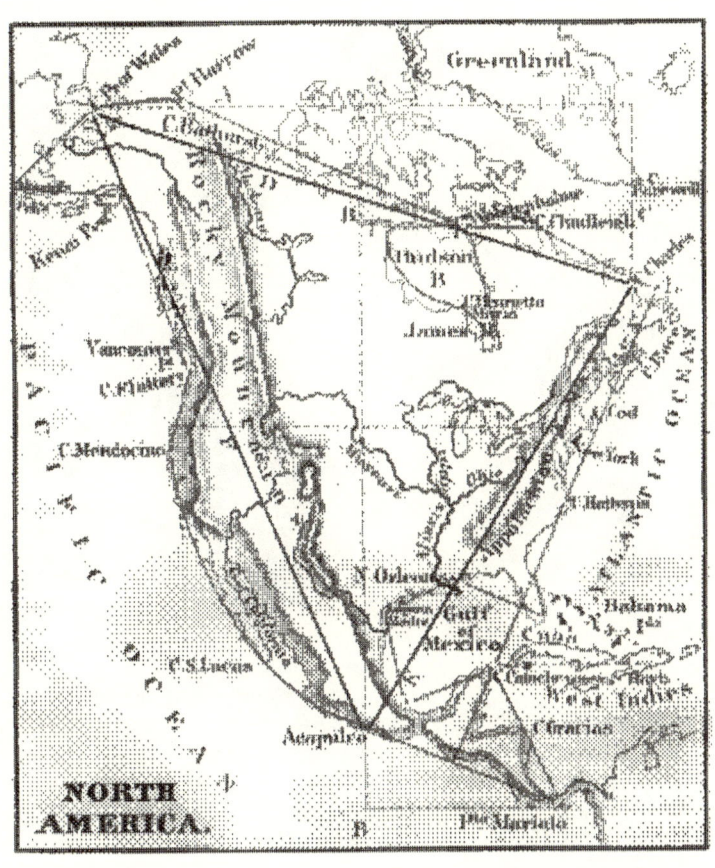

NORTH
AMERICA.

Mark *Cape Prince of Wales* at its west end, and *Cape Charles* at its east end.

2. From the point where B crosses D, measure six times the length of M southward; and, a little above the point found, mark *Acapulco*.

3. From Acapulco draw E and F to Cape Prince of Wales and Cape Charles. We now have the triangle, which includes the greater part of the continent, and which may be called the *General* or *Fundamental* form.

APPROXIMATE FORM.—1. Divide D and E each into three equal parts. We thus find on D *Cape Parry*, near *Cape Bathurst;* and *Southampton* Island, near *Cape Wolstenholme.* On E *New Orleans;* and near the upper division, *New York.*

II. PACIFIC COAST.—1. From the upper point on E, near New York, trace a horizontal line G to the left, making its length four M. A little below the end of this line is *Cape Mendocino*, which is about midway between Cape Prince of Wales and Acapulco.

2. Draw one M from Cape Mendocino toward Cape Bathurst. At the end is the southern part of *Vancouver's Island;* and a very little below is *Cape Flattery.*

From Cape Flattery draw two M toward Cape Prince of Wales, and mark *Kenai Peninsula.* From this point draw, to the left, a horizontal line one and one-quarter M. This is the line of *Aliaska* Peninsula. Draw a line from the end of it to Cape Prince of Wales.

3. Join Cape Mendocino to Acapulco by a regular curve, which divide into three equal parts. At the lower division is *Cape San Lucas*, and near the upper division is the head of *Gulf of California.* This curve, with the lines between it and Cape Prince of Wales, gives the *Pacific Coast* as far south as Acapulco.

4. Extend the line B from Acapulco one M, and draw a horizontal line to the right a little more than two ($2\frac{1}{2}$) M. We thus find *Punta Mariato,* the most southern point of the continent. Join this to Acapulco, and we have the Pacific Coast of *Central America.*

III. ATLANTIC COAST.—1. From Acapulco on this last line, measure one M. From Cape Charles continue the line D one-fourth M, and mark L. Join this point to the point at the right of Acapulco. This is the line of *Atlantic Coast.*

2. From L measure on this line one-half M, mark *Cape Ray.* From Cape Ray on the same line, we find, 1, *Cape Cod ;* 2, *Cape Hatteras ;* 3, middle of *Florida ;* 4, *Cape Catoche ;* 5, coast of the *Pacific ;* each distant one M from the next. Join Punta Mariato to Cape Catoche; and, on this line, one M from Punta Mariato, mark *Cape Gracias.*

3. *Gulf of Mexico.*—From Cape Catoche draw one M toward Acapulco. From the end of it draw one M upward, slanting a little to the left, and mark *Laguna Madre.* From the line B opposite this point, draw a horizontal line to the right, two M in length ; at its end is *southeast point of Florida (Turkey Point).* Join Laguna Madre, New Orleans, and Turkey Point. From this last point draw a line to meet the line L, a little above middle of Florida.

IV. ARCTIC COAST.—1. From Southampton Island draw a horizontal line to the right one M in length. At its end mark *Cape Chudleigh.* Join this to Cape Charles and Cape Wolstenholme.

2. One M to the right of Cape Prince of Wales, mark *Point Barrow,* and join it to Cape Prince of Wales and Southampton Island.

3. *Hudson Bay.*—Three-fourths M to the left of Southampton is the northwest corner of Hudson Bay, mark L. A little less than one M directly below Cape Wolstenholme mark *Cape Henrietta Maria.* Through this point draw a line from I, a little less than two M in length. At its end is the southern point of *James Bay.* Join this point to Cape Wolstenholme and to Cape Henrietta Maria ; by a curve join Cape Henrietta Maria to I.

We have now all the important points on the entire coast joined by straight or curved lines. This gives us very nearly the true form of the continent. We may therefore call it the *Approximate Form.* We have now only to join these points by the bending coast line, noticing in each case how it differs from the straight lines.

ISLANDS.—1. *The West Indies.* From Cape Catoche draw to the right a horizontal line, two M in length ; and there mark east end of *Hayti.* At half that distance is the east part of *Cuba,* and a little below is *Jamaica.* From the east end of Hayti a slanting line to the middle of Florida gives the direction of the *Bahamas.*

2. Above Cape Charles, on the vertical line, we find Cape Farewell, nearly one M distant. Half one M to the right of B, and half one M above A mark the entrance of *Smith's Strait*. These two points enable us to draw *Greenland*.

3. We have already Cape Ray, the southern point of *Newfoundland*. One half M to the right and a little above, is Cape *Race*, its eastern point.

INTERNAL CONSTRUCTION.

1. MOUNTAINS.—1. The *Rocky Mountains* and their prolongation form almost a straight line from the mouth of the Mackenzie to the isthmus of Tehuantepec. Opposite Cape Mendocino they turn eastward, and then directly south, leaving just one-third the width of the continent west of them at *Long's Peak*. Opposite the mouth of the Colorado, they return to their original southeast direction.

2. Another system of mountains extends parallel with the coast from the peninsula of Aliaska to the isthmus of Panama. The principal range is the *Sierra Nevada*.

3. A smaller system, the *Appalachians*, extends in curves from the mouth of the St. Lawrence nearly to the Gulf of Mexico. Their general direction is from the northeast to the southwest. They lie opposite the middle of the western system, and extend through only a part of the length of the coast.

II. RIVERS AND LAKES.—*The Mississippi and its Tributaries.*—
1. Measure from New Orleans one M (the *measure* used in drawing the coast) directly above, and we find the mouth of the *Missouri* ; one more gives us the northwest shore of *Lake Superior* ; and a little to the left of this, we find *Lake Itasca*, the source of the Mississippi, after which we can easily draw the river.

2. From the mouth of the Missouri one M directly northwest, brings us to the point where the Missouri leaves the Rocky Mountains, very near its source. The *Platte* leaves the Rocky Mountains at their great southern bend, flowing almost directly east. The *Arkansas* is one-half M farther south, and enters the Mississippi midway between the Missouri and its mouth. The *Red River* flows from

4

the highland one-half M south of the Arkansas, and is nearly parallel with it.

3. The *mouth* of the *Ohio* is nearly opposite Cape Hatteras, and its *source* is in the Appalachian Mountains nearly opposite New York.

4. From the point which we found on Lake Superior, one M toward New York gives us *Niagara*, and half way between these two points is the *junction* of the greatest three Lakes. From these three points we easily draw the Lakes and the St. Lawrence.*

5. One-half M west of Point Bathurst is the *mouth* of the *Mackenzie*. In the Rocky Mountains, at Mount Brown, two measures from the mouth of the Mackenzie, we find the *source* of that river. The lower half of its course is parallel to the mountains. The upper half is nearly a half circle. The upper course is called *Athabasca*. On the top of this curve we find *Athabasca Lake*. About one-third the distance to the sea is *Great Slave Lake*, and at another third, *Great Bear Lake*.

6. Near the source of the Mackenzie is that of the *Saskatchewan*, which flows nearly east into the Hudson Bay. At the point in its course nearest to the source of the Mississippi, we find *Lake Winnipeg*. From this lake to the mouth, the river is called the *Nelson*.

7. At the Great Bend of the Rocky Mountains, toward the east, is *Union Peak*, the source of the greatest two of the Pacific rivers. The *Colorado* flows southwest to the Gulf of California; and the south branch of the *Columbia* northwest, entering the sea south of Cape Flattery.

6. The *Rio Grande del Norte* has its source in the Rocky Mountains, very near that of the Arkansas; and its mouth is just midway between that of the Mississippi and the Isthmus of Tehuantepec.

8. The *Yukon*, which corresponds to this at the other end of the mountains, has its source opposite the great bend of the Mackenzie, and its mouth directly above the neck of the Aliaska peninsula. These two streams and the Saskatchewan are all about the same length,

* We can avoid mistakes by noticing that the northwest shore of Lake Superior and the southeast of Lake Erie are nearly parallel, and distant just one M from each other; and that the same distance separates the head of Lake Michigan from the foot of Lake Ontario.

not much shorter than one and two-thirds M. The space between the source of the Mackenzie and that of the Rio Grande is but one-fourth of the length of the mountain system, and yet all the great rivers of the continent, except the Yukon and St. Lawrence, rise within that space.

10. The Atlantic rivers are easily drawn, because all flow from the Appalachian Mountains. Most of them have a nearly straight course—those north of the Susquehanna flowing south; those south of it, east and southeast.

CHARACTERISTIC STRUCTURE OF THE CONTINENT.

A continent is not simply a piece of land, detached from a homogeneous general mass, but it has a special structure, great features of relief—mountains, table-lands, and plains—arranged according to a plan which belongs to it alone, and which is distinct from the plan of every other continent. This plan of the continent comprises all its parts, and none can be displaced without changing its entire character. To exhibit this characteristic plan of structure, and thus render the geography of the continent intelligible, is the purpose of Guyot's *Physical Wall Atlas*.

The characteristic features of the structure of North America are the immense highland region on the west, which forms half the entire continent; the lesser highland region of the east; the great central plain, resulting from the prolonged inner slopes of these two highland regions; the two large inland seas; and the combination of the greater portion of the continental waters into a few great systems.

I. The two highland regions approaching each other at the south, without meeting each other, and diverging on the north, give the continent its characteristic triangular form. The fact of their being separated at the south by a great depression, permits the formation, by the Atlantic, of that great Mediterranean, the Gulf of Mexico, to which the whole eastern half of the continent owes its fertility.

The meeting of their two inner slopes marks the greatest depression between them, and gives the Mississippi River its position far eastward of the centre of the continent; and the falling of this same depression below the level of the sea, as it does where the highland regions are most widely separated, gives to the continent its great northern Mediterranean, the Hudson Bay.

The prolongation of the western highlands from northwest to southeast, gives the Pacific coast its great extension in that direction; and the continuity of this highland region causes the almost unbroken line of the Pacific coast. The one narrow Mediterranean of this coast, the Gulf of California, is permitted only by a short break in the outlying mountains which skirt the main mass of the highland throughout its entire extent. The sea is thus permitted to enter and fill the valley lying between the outlying mountains and the main mass, but its progress toward the interior of the continent is effectually barred by the latter. The same is true of the smaller indentations of this coast, San Francisco Bay and the Strait of Juan de Fuca. These are but a few of the influences exerted upon the character of this continent by the character and relative position of its two main features of relief. Others will appear in their order.

II. The vast western or Pacific highland region is the main axis of the continent and its most controlling feature. All that is characteristic of the continent is in a greater or less degree allied to it. This highland region consists of a broad, high, and mountainous plateau, with the Rocky Mountains resting on the eastern and higher side; and the Sierra Nevada, Cascade, and lower mountains, on the western edge. The plateau is of nearly equal width in every part, except in the middle portion, opposite Cape Mendocino, where its general width is nearly doubled.

At this point, the highlands obtain a breadth of not less than 1,500 miles. The Sierra Nevada and Rocky Mountains are separated by not less than 700 miles of plateau.

East of the Rocky Mountains there is a long, gentle slope to the middle of the continent, the Great Western Plains. West of the Sierra Nevada there is but a very short, rapid slope to the sea.

Both the plateau and the mountains upon it are quite low in the north; but both increase in height toward the south, to the middle and broadest part of the highland region. Here the average elevation of the base of the Rocky Mountains is not less than 6,000 feet. The average height of the two ranges is about 12,000 feet; while the highest peaks attain an elevation of 14,000 to 15,000 feet, and are covered permanently with snow.

From this point southward, the mountains gradually become lower and disappear; but the plateau, on the whole, continues gradually to increase in height, to the region between Vera Cruz and Acapulco, where it attains its greatest elevation. Here the plateau is surmounted by numerous high volcanic peaks, among which is Popocatepetl, the highest mountain of North America. From this point the descent is constant and rapid through Central America to the Isthmus of Panama.

III. The eastern, or *Atlantic* highland, is very much shorter—only about one-third the length of the western—and also much narrower. Unlike the Pacific highland, this region is separated into two parts by the broad valley of the St. Lawrence—the *Appalachian* system of mountains, along the eastern coast, and the *highlands of Canada and Labrador* north of the St. Lawrence.

The Appalachian system, also called the Alleghanies, consists mainly of several low mountain ranges, side by side, and nearly parallel. They are not broken into wild peaks, like the Rocky and Sierra Nevada Mountains, but the ranges have rounded and uniform summits, and seem like long folds of the earth's surface. The western part of the system, however, is more in the form of a plateau, which gradually descends toward the interior of the continent.

The Appalachian mountain system is also broken entirely across by the valley of the Hudson and Mohawk, which affords easy access from the Atlantic seaboard of the United States to the interior of the continent.

Again, the average elevation of this mountain system is not more than 2,000 to 3,000 feet, while its highest summits reach an elevation of 6,000. Thus we perceive a most marked contrast between these two main highland regions of the continent. The predominant character of the western is that of immense plateaus; of the eastern is that of parallel mountain ranges. The western is of vast extent, the eastern is comparatively small. The western is of great height, and forms an unbroken mass from the Arctic Ocean to the Isthmus of Tehuantepec. The eastern is low, and is broken entirely across by two valleys, through both of which easy access is obtained into the heart of the continent.

IV. The great interior plain, formed by the prolonged inner slopes of the highland regions, is crossed in the middle by a low swell, called the *Height of Land*, which connects the Atlantic and the Pacific highlands. It is thus divided into two parts, one sloping toward the Arctic Sea; the other toward the Gulf of Mexico. This central swell is very slight, being only from 1,500 to 1,600 feet in elevation about the sources of the Mississippi, and 1,000 feet in its lowest depression. Its slopes, and those toward the highlands on each side of the plain, are so gradual that we might travel from the shores of the Arctic Ocean to the Gulf of Mexico, and from the eastern side of the plain to the western, and be hardly aware of a difference in altitudes.

V. The Rocky Mountain system is the main water-shed of the continent, and nearly all the great rivers of the continent rise in the limited portion of the system situated between Long's Peak and Mount Brown. This mountain system really marks the culmination of the continent, from which there is a general descent eastward to the Atlantic, and westward to the Pacific.

The general eastward slope is interrupted by the comparatively slight elevation of the Atlantic highlands. The western slope is maintained at nearly the same general level from the base of the mountains to the Sierra Nevada, beyond which the descent to the Pacific is rapid. This conformation of the continent is beautifully exhibited by the profiles at the bottom of the map. A to A' exhibits the elevations of the continent traversed by a line extending from Cape Charles across the highlands of Labrador and the central plain to Mount Brown, thence across the Pacific highlands to Cape Flattery. B to B' exhibits the elevations across the continent from Cape Hatteras to St. Louis, thence across the Pacific highlands, by way of Denver and Great Salt Lake Cities, to San Francisco. In looking at these profiles, we are at once struck with the comparative insignificance of the Atlantic highlands, and the almost unbroken continuity of the slope from the base of the Rocky Mountains to the Atlantic. We also notice that the western slope is sufficiently apparent, though it is less apparent than the eastern, on account of the almost uniform elevation of that portion of the plateau between the Rocky Mountains and the Sierra Nevada. The more marked character, the greater breadth and elevation of the central portion of the highland region, is also apparent on a comparison of these two profiles.

These slopes of the continent being thus distinctly marked, the division of the falling waters at the Rocky Mountains is as natural and as easy to comprehend as is the division of those which fall upon the roof of a house by the central ridge, which forms two opposing slopes in the roof. As flowing waters invariably follow the slope of the land from the higher to the lower level, we at once judge that the general direction of the flowing waters by the slope of the Rocky Mountains will be eastward, and at right angles to the dividing line, while those on the western slope will flow westward.

An examination of the map shows at once that our conclusion is a correct one. All the streams rising on the eastern slope of these mountains flow eastward in a general direction at right angles to the direction of the mountain system, continuing this course throughout the highest portions of the slope. We remark, however, that from about the meridian of 100° W. Lon., all the streams within the limit of the United States depart from their original direction and turn toward the south; while those in British America, as near the mountains as the 110th meridian, tend toward the north. Let us seek the solution of this.

An examination of the profile B to B′ shows that from the mountains to the terrace near the meridian of 100° W. Lon., the slope is more rapid, and thence diminishes toward the Mississippi. It will be remembered, also, that a swell, called the Height of Land, which is some 1,600 feet in elevation, extends across the central plain, in the region of the great lakes, and dividing the plain into a northern and a southern slope. Where the slope from the Rocky Mountains becomes more gradual and is more nearly equal to that from the central swell, the latter begins to manifest its influence on the flowing waters. The slope from this swell impels them southward, while that from the western highlands impels them eastward, and thus they take a direction between the two, that is, a southeast course.

At the meridian of 90° their course is again changed, and they go directly southward, and are therefore all combined into one stream. If we seek the explanation of this, we find it in the fact that, along this line, they encounter the ascending slope to the Atlantic highlands, which, slight as it is, is yet sufficient to prevent their further progress eastward, and they now obey alone the force which impels them southward. If we trace now the influence of the secondary watershed of the continent, the Atlantic highlands, we find that, on the same principle, the streams which rise on its western slope are impelled westward and southwestward until they reach the line where the ascending slope to the western highlands leaves them free to follow the southward tendency alone. Here they are blended with the streams descending from the western highlands, and from the Height of Land, and help to form the great Mississippi.

No other combination of the flowing waters of this portion of the continent is possible while the relief of the continent remains the same; nor can we conceive the possibility, with this arrangement of the slopes, of the formation of the Mississippi elsewhere than in the position it occupies, namely, along the line in which the inner slopes of the two highlands meet.

The formation of the Hudson Bay system of rivers from a portion of the streams of the Rocky Mountains, together with those from the highlands of Labrador and the northern slope of the central plain, is accounted for by a corresponding action of the surrounding slopes.

The Mackenzie system is formed farther north, where, by the descent northward of the Pacific highlands, and the swell of the Arctic highlands, on the east, the waters are forced to the north.

The St. Lawrence system is formed in a slight depression between the broad, nearly uniform swell of the Height of Land, and the Atlantic highlands, through which the flowing waters find a natural outlet to the ocean.

The greater portion of the flowing waters of the continent are thus, under the influence of the peculiar and characteristic forms of relief, combined into four great river systems. The rivers rising on the outer slopes of the two systems of highlands find a short and generally quite direct course to the sea, and are very little combined. We thus perceive that, while a system of mountains is sufficient to give the original direction to the streams which have their source upon it, their subsequent direction, and their combination into systems, is due to the *general arrangement of surface elevations.* It is obvious, therefore, that, in order to comprehend correctly the drainage of a continent, a knowledge of its general surface elevation, or forms of relief, is of preöminent importance. The absolute necessity for this knowledge will be still more apparent when we study in detail the drainage of the United States.

E. The influence of the physical conformation of the continent upon its supply of moisture, and, therefore, upon its capabilities in the hands of a civilized community, are equally as marked as upon the distribution of the continental waters.

The meridian of 98°, passing along the extreme western limits of the Gulf of Mexico and Hudson Bay, divides the main body of the continent into two regions, which, as far north as the latitude of 50°, are utterly unlike in character. The prevailing winds in this portion of the continent are from the west and southwest. The eastern region lies in the path of the winds which sweep over the Gulf of Mexico, and which carry with them abundant supplies of moisture from the warm waters. It therefore has frequent rains throughout the entire year, and in consequence has a rich vegetation. The dense growth of forests which, little more than a century ago, covered this entire region, except in the extreme west, is well known. This section of the continent is thus admirably adapted to all occupations which require a fertile soil and the ready growth of plants.

The Pacific highlands differ from the eastern regions in being very dry. The moisture which the prevailing winds would bring to them from the Pacific is nearly all taken away by the cold Sierra Nevada and Cascade Mountains, against which they strike. Consequently very little rain falls in all this region, except on the mountains and on the coast regions west of the Sierra Nevada and the Cascade range.

The mountains and their valleys, which receive the rain, are covered with forests like those of the east. The valleys of California

4°

and Oregon are justly celebrated on account of their great wealth of vegetation.

The broad plateau which forms the mass of this highland region is, however, entirely without trees, except rare ones on the mountain slopes; and but for a few kinds of low gray plants, called sages, which are hardly distinguishable on the dry, gray soil, it would be quite a desert.

In all this great highland region, therefore, agriculture is nearly impossible, except on the borders of streams, in the mountain valleys, and in the valleys of the Pacific slope.

The main resource of all this vast region is, therefore, its mineral wealth. This, however, is sufficient to have already attracted a large and rapidly-increasing population in many portions of the country, even where a supply of food from the inhospitable soil is entirely out of the question.

Between this dry, treeless, western region and the forests of the east, is a region subject to occasional summer droughts, yet having moisture sufficient to secure great fertility. Here trees are found only on the borders of the streams, or on the low hills that here and there break the monotonous level of the plain. This is the region of the prairies, celebrated for their luxuriant growth of grass, and their abundant harvests of wheat and corn.

North of lat. 50° this great contrast between the east and the west is no longer apparent. A belt of forests crosses the entire continent, extending, on the west coast, much further northward than in the east, or even in the interior. In the east, the forests are scarcely found north of Cape Charles; while in the west they extend even to Aliaska. The difference in temperature indicated by this difference in vegetation is due in the main to the prevailing winds. Icy Arctic winds, blowing from the northeast, prevail in the east; while the west is favored with the comparatively warm winds from the Pacific. The difference due to these causes is, however, considerably enhanced by the floating masses of ice from the Arctic, and the cold ocean currents, that chill the coast of Labrador, neither of which exist on the Pacific coasts. The elevation also of the Arctic coasts and the mass of Arctic islands, has undoubtedly a considerable influence in depressing the temperature of the northeastern region of the continent.

· To realize still better the influence of the structure of the continent upon its entire character, we have but to suppose any one feature blotted out, or changed in position, and we shall find that an entire change in the character of the continent would be the result. Suppose the Atlantic highlands were continued southward along the Atlantic coast to a junction with the Yucatan peninsula, no Gulf of Mexico would exist, and the east, losing its principal source of moisture, would be almost as barren as the great western plains. Suppose the two highland regions, having precisely the same structure they now have, were placed in the reverse position to that which they now occupy, the two parts of the continent would then be of an opposite character; for the Sierra Nevada and Rocky Mountains, lying parallel with the course of the winds, instead of at right angles to them, as they now do, would then offer no obstacle to the distribution of moisture over the entire plateau; while the low Appalachian Mountains would have presented no considerable barrier to the entrance of a wealth of moisture and warmth from the warm vapor-laden winds of the Pacific.

We cannot doubt that, with such a change—with the high, unbroken barrier of the Pacific highlands shutting out the great civilized nations of the Old World from access to the interior, a corresponding change in the destinies of this continent would have taken place.

A glance at the political geography of the continent can but confirm this view. The contrast between the eastern and the western regions being what it is, we are not surprised to find that almost the entire population of the main body of the continent is gathered in the former, and in the broad fertile valleys west of the Sierra Nevada and the Cascade Mountains. Great numbers of cities and towns have grown up in the east, the largest being at those points where access is most direct to the productive interior. *New York* is at the entrance to the great natural passage across the Appalachian highlands, and commands the most practicable route from the Atlantic seaboard to the fertile West. It owes its commercial importance to this position, which makes it the most available port for the shipment of our great agricultural staples from the interior plains to Europe.

Chicago, by its position at the extreme end of the route to the interior, becomes the purchasing and forwarding agent of New York, and hence its rapid growth and great commercial importance. *New Orleans*, by its position at the mouth of the Mississippi, commands ready access to the entire Mississippi basin. *Cincinnati* and *St. Louis* occupy the same position in reference to the great southern mart which Chicago occupies in reference to New York; and before their connection with the Atlantic ports by railroad, their relations to New Orleans were much the same as is that of Chicago to New York.

Philadelphia, Baltimore, and Boston are the centres of commerce more or less allied to the great manufacturing interests of the States in the northeastern portions of the Appalachian Mountain region. The great importance of manufacturing in this section of our country is due to the admirable facilities for this occupation afforded by the valuable water-power of the streams, and the rich mineral deposits of this mountain region; combined with its somewhat sterile soil and cold climate, which discourage agriculture in a number of those States.

San Francisco, the only considerable city of the Pacific seaboard, has grown up within the last twenty years, solely on account of the access afforded by its bay, and the two streams flowing together into it, to the gold-bearing Sierra Nevada.

Montreal and *Quebec*, the largest cities of British America, are on the St. Lawrence, the only doorway possessed by England to her vast territories in the interior of the continent.

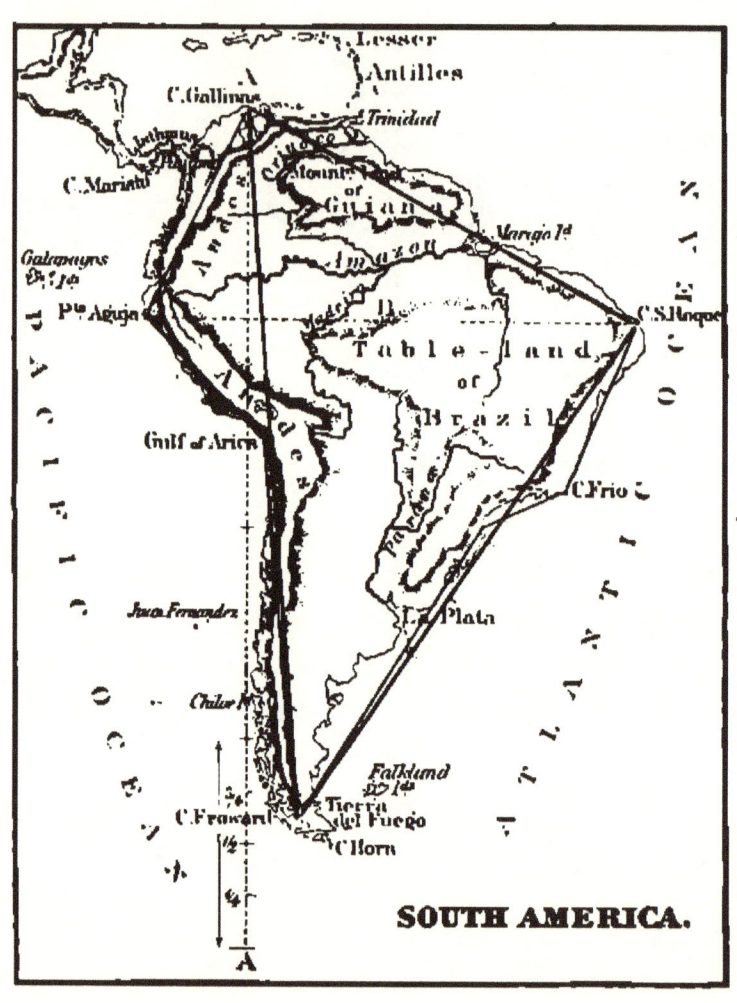

SOUTH AMERICA.

SOUTH AMERICA.

LINES OF CONSTRUCTION.—1. Draw, at the left of the middle of the slate or paper, a vertical line, A, and divide it into four *equal* parts.

2. Through the upper point of division draw a horizontal line, B, making its length at the *left*, half of one division of A; and at the *right* nearly double one division. These are the lines of construction.

FUNDAMENTAL FORM.—1. Mark at the top of A, *Cape Gallinas;* and at the right hand end of B, *Cape St. Roque.*

2. A little to the right of the middle of the lower quarter of A, mark *Cape Froward.*

3. Join these three capes, and we have the triangle which makes the fundamental form of the continent.

APPROXIMATE FORM.—1. At the left end of the horizontal line, B, mark *Punta Aguja.*

2. Mark the middle of that quarter of the vertical line which is next below B. A little below and to the right of this point, mark the *Gulf of Arica.*

3. Join Cape Gallinas, Punta Aguja, Gulf of Arica, and Cape Froward.

4. Divide the southeast line of the fundamental form into *three* equal parts.

5. A little to the right of the upper point of division, mark *Cape Frio;* and at about the same distance, directly above the lower point, mark the mouth of the *La Plata.*

6. Divide the middle one of these thirds again into three equal parts; and, opposite the upper point of division, within the line, mark *Gulf of Paranagua.* (This is the point at which the coast, after going nearly west from Cape Frio, turns again southward.) Its

distance from the line should be the same as that of Cape Frio, and the mouth of the La Plata.

7. Join Cape Froward, Gulf of Paranagua, Cape Frio, and Cape St. Roque. We now have the *approximate* form of the continent.

(If the map is held with the bottom upward, it will appear to be a sort of monument, with a four-sided figure for its base, and a pyramid for its top, with gently sloping lines joining them.)

TRUE FORM.—We have now only to connect these points with the proper coast lines.

To assist in drawing the northern coast, notice that the mouth of the Orinoco is a little farther south than Cape Gallinas, and at a distance from it equal to that from Punta Aguja to the vertical line ; that the mouth of the Amazon is just half way between that of the Orinoco and Cape St. Roque; and that the junction of the Isthmus of Panama is directly west of the mouth of the Orinoco, at a distance equal to that of the mouth of the Amazon.

Notice on the eastern coast, south of the mouth of the La Plata, that two projections divide that part of the coast into three nearly equal parts. Other divisions of this kind can be found to guide the drawing between most of the principal points.

III.—*Structure of the Continent.*

The continent of South America has for its main axis the long chain of the Andes, which extends in the main from north to south, with two great bends in the northern portion. The north and south direction of this axis gives to the continent its proper elongation in the same direction, and its continuity connects together all portions of the continent. Its situation, on the extreme western border, makes the continent one-sided, depriving it of a western domain which might counterpoise the eastern as does the western domain. of the North American continent. Its elevation bars nearly the whole continent from access to the Pacific.

This main highland system in the west, the extended but comparatively low table-lands of Brazil in the east, the smaller mountainous region of Guyana on the north, and the great central plain along the foot of the Andes and between the eastern highlands, with its three great river systems, constitute the fundamental features of the continental structure. This structure is especially characteristic of South America, and is not repeated in any other continent. Even when compared with its sister continent, North America, whose general plan of structure is the same, the differences are striking.

In South America the western highlands assume the form of a high and comparatively narrow mountain system, the base of which does not exceed 200 or 300 miles in width. In the western highlands of North America the table-land form predominates, and they expand to the enormous breadth of 1,500 to 2,000 miles. The respective elevation of these two highland regions is not less different. The average elevation of the peaks of the Rocky Mountains and the Sierra Nevada scarcely reaches the bottom of the high valleys or plateaus of the Andes, from which peaks rise 8,000 or 10,000 feet higher.

Nor are the western highlands of North America so close to the border of the continent. Between them and the Pacific are the broad and fertile valleys of California and Oregon with space sufficient for rich and powerful states.

In the eastern highland, the Plateau of Brazil, which corresponds to the Appalachian Mountain system of North America, the table-land form greatly predominates; and though the position in the continent and the general elevation of these two highland regions is the same, that of South America is of much the greater extent.

Though the frozen heights of Labrador and the Arctic highlands, in the north continent, represent, in some measure, the mountain land of Guyana, the difference in the influence which they exert upon the continent to which they belong is obvious.

Again, though the three main streams of South America, the Amazon, the La Plata, and the Orinoco, have their corresponding streams in the Saskatchewan, Mississippi, and Mackenzie, their relative importance is altogether different.

The Amazon, of South America, the greatest of rivers, corresponds in position to the Saskatchewan, which is not even second or third among the streams of North America. The La Plata occupies the second place in South American streams; the Mississippi first in those of North America. The Orinoco is third in South America; the Mackenzie second among North American streams. The St. Lawrence also occupies in its continent a much higher rank than the San Francisco, the corresponding stream in South America.

The climatic situation of South America, which makes it a tropical continent, distinguishes it completely in regard to the vegetable and animal life, from its congener, the continent of North America. The special structure described, combined with this climatic situation, makes South America again, by the superabundance of moisture and of vegetable life, entirely different from the other tropical continents. Its position, between the tropics and on both sides of the equator, places it in the path of both the northeast and the southeast trade-winds, which sweep over it during the entire year. The Serra do Mar and the Serra Espinaço, on the eastern portion of the plateau of Brazil, are the only obstacles which these winds meet until they reach the Andes. Thus every portion of the main mass of the continent, east of the Andes, except the inner portion of the plateau of Brazil, is constantly bathed by these moisture-laden winds. The result is that torrents of rain fall during the wet season, and during the dry season are deposited, each night, dews so copious as almost to be equivalent to showers.

As a consequence of this tropical temperature and abundant moisture, all this portion of South America boasts a wealth of vegetation unrivalled except in the Indies, which have a corresponding climatic condition. The luxuriance of vegetation on the plains of the Amazon and in the coast regions of Brazil is too well known to require description. In what marked contrast with these regions are the scanty forests and meagre prairies of the inner part of the Brazilian plateau, which the ocean winds reach only after being robbed of a great part of their moisture by the mountain chains near the coast, and the dryness of which is aggravated by its plateau character!

Again, the narrow coast regions of Peru and Bolivia, which lie west of the Andes, are entirely rainless, and almost deserts. Lying

In that portion of the continent in which east and southeast winds prevail, their rains must come from the Atlantic; but the Atlantic winds are deprived of all moisture in their passage over the Andes, and thus they have no rain to give this region.

A little farther to the south, outside the tropical regions, where the return trades commence blowing from the Pacific, we find the fertile and beautiful lands of Chili, west of the Andes; while the parched pampas and the dreary desert of Patagonia, on the east, attest again the influence of this mountain barrier.

No one of these fundamental features of the structure of South America can be destroyed or displaced without changing the peculiar nature of this continent. Suppose the Andes, remaining the same high, continuous mountain system they now are, were placed along the eastern coast, opposing the course of the trade-winds, and condensing all their vapors. The whole continent at the west, except the narrow southern portion, would become comparatively parched, and its wealth of vegetation and animal life would be no more. That southern portion, instead of being the waste it now is, would be moist and fertile like Chili.

Suppose the plateau of Brazil to be lowered to the level of the plains, the striking contrast between the moist climate and luxuriant vegetation of the coast region, and the dryness of the climate and scantiness of the vegetation of the plateau, would cease to exist. The relative usefulness to man, and the change in the destinies of the continent, which would follow these physical changes, is evident. No modification, therefore, could be made in the size, form, or relative situation of any part of the continent without effecting a corresponding change in the whole.

If we consider the distribution of the population of South America, we find, as in North America, a remarkable connection between it and the physical character of the continent.

Almost the entire civilized population of Brazil is gathered in the coast regions. *Rio Janeiro*, the largest city of the continent, is situated on a fine harbor, nearly under the Tropic of Capricorn, at that point on the coast from which access is most easily obtained to the gold and diamond regions of the interior. *Bahia*, the second city of Brazil, is situated on another fine bay, farther to the north. Both those cities are surrounded by regions rich in all the agricultural products of fertile tropical lands.

In the Argentine Republic, the larger part of which is occupied by the pampas, the civilized population is gathered along the La Plata and Parana. The interior is abandoned to the half-savage Gauchos, whose only occupation is the little care they bestow upon the herds which roam at will over the grassy plains, and constitute almost the entire wealth of the country. Buenos Ayres, at the mouth of the Parana, is one of the leading commercial cities of South America, but we should not be surprised to find that its commerce is confined principally to the trade in hides, horns, and tallow.

In Venezuela, the Llanos of the Orinoco, reduced to a desert during half the year, are occupied only by herdsmen and herds like those of the pampas. The climate of the lowlands being exceedingly hot and partially unhealthful, the sedentary population is gathered principally in the highlands; and the capital and largest city, Caracas, is situated among the mountains at some distance from the coast.

In the tropical States of the Pacific—Colombia, Ecuador, Peru, and Bolivia—the larger part of the population is gathered in the high valleys of the Andes, notwithstanding the difficulty of access under which they often labor. The fine climate, due to their elevation, gives them greatly the advantage over the lowlands, which, though exceedingly fertile, are also, for the most part, insalubrious. In Bolivia and Peru many valleys, which are so high and cold as to be almost entirely unproductive, and which can have no communication with the lower and more fertile valleys, except by routes practicable only for the sure-footed mule and llama, yet boast of fine cities, gathered there solely by the mineral wealth of these inhospitable heights. Without this mineral wealth these mountain heights would never have been scaled, and Cuzco, Potosi, Sucre, and La Paz would have had no existence. Remove the Andes of Colombia and Ecuador from a tropical to a temperate region, and the now beautiful and fertile valleys of Popayan, Bogota, and Quito, 5,000, 8,000, and 9,000 feet above the level of the sea, would be almost uninhabitable.

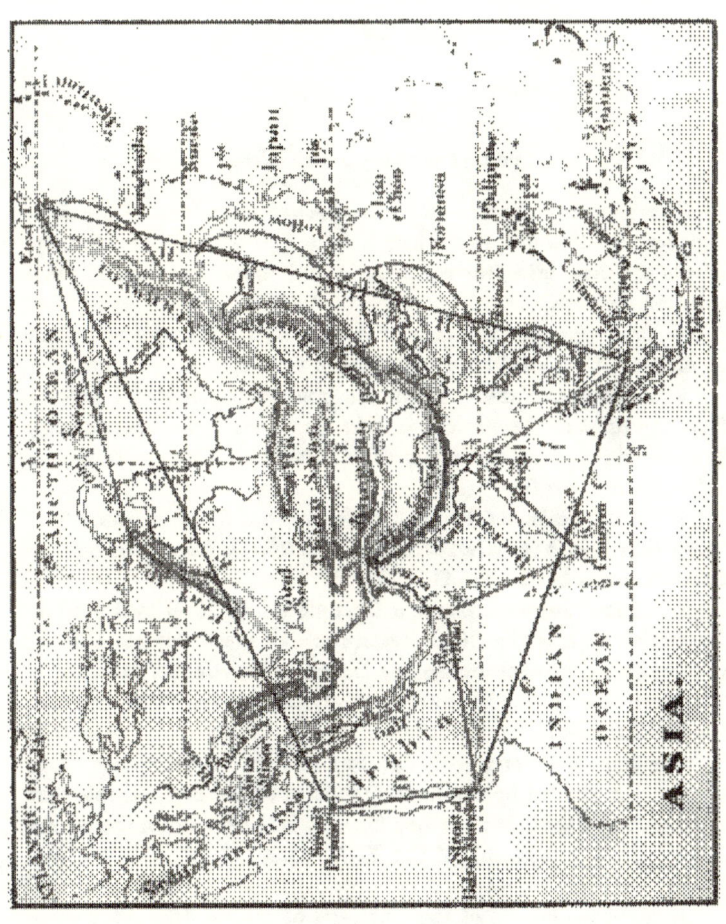

ASIA.

ASIA.

CONSTRUCTION LINES.—1. Draw through the middle of the slate, or paper, a *vertical* line, A, the length desired for the height of the map. Divide this line into *four* equal parts, and mark one part M for a common measure.

2. Draw through both ends of the line A, and through each point of division, *horizontal* lines, which mark 1, 2, 3, 4, 5.

FUNDAMENTAL FORM.—1. On the uppermost horizontal line, $1\frac{3}{4}$ M to the right of the vertical, is *East Cape*. On the lowermost, $\frac{3}{4}$ M to the right of the vertical, is *Cape Romania*. Connect these two points by the line B.

2. On the horizontal line 4, *a little less* than $2\frac{1}{4}$ M to the left of the vertical line, is the strait of *Bab-el-Mandeb*. Connect this point to Cape Romania by the line C.

3. On the horizontal line 3, *a little more* than $2\frac{1}{4}$ M to the left of the vertical line, is the *Sinai Peninsula*. Connect this point to the strait of Bab-el-Mandeb by the line D, and to East Cape by the line E. We have now the fundamental form of Asia, which is an irregular four-sided figure.

APPROXIMATE FORM.—1. The line B, from East Cape to Cape Romania, is divided by the horizontal lines which meet it, into four equal parts. Just below the line 2, on B, is the mouth of the *Amoor River*. At 3 is the head of the *Yellow Sea*. At 4 is the *coast of China* near *Hainan*.

2. Mark the middle of the four parts of B, and draw upon them the four curves which you see on the model.

3. On the fourth horizontal line, and in the vertical line A, is the head of the *Gulf of Bengal*. Connect Cape Romania to this point.

4. A little below and to the right of the middle of C, is *Cape Comorin*. Connect it to the Gulf of Bengal.

5. One M to the left of the Gulf of Bengal, and a little above (one-fifth M), is the *mouth of the Indus*. Connect it to Cape Comorin and Bab-el-Mandeb.

6. At the point where the north slanting line E crosses the second horizontal line, draw a line a little less than half M at right angles to the line E. At its end is the *northern termination of the Ural Mountains.*

7. Divide the left-hand portion of this slanting line E, into three equal parts. The right-hand point of division gives us the *south end of the Ural Mountains.* The left point is the middle of the chain of the *Caucasus.*

8. Connect the south and north ends of the Ural Mountains, and the latter point to the East Cape.

TRUE FORM.—We now have the approximate form of the continent, except the two small projections, *Kamtchatka* and *Corea,* on the east coast ; *Asia Minor,* between the Caucasus and Sinai Peninsula ; and *Northeast Cape,* near the Gulf of Obi. By surrounding this approximate form with the proper coast lines, and adding these projections in their proper forms and places, as seen on the model, the true form of the continent is obtained.

To assist in drawing the true form, notice that the south end of *Kamtchatka* is almost directly below East Cape, and does not quite reach the second horizontal line. *Corea* is on the third horizontal line. The head of the *Gulf of Siam* is about midway from Cape Romania to the Gulf of Bengal. *Ras-el-Had,* east point of Arabia, is about one-third the distance from the mouth of the Indus to Bab-el-Mandeb. Half the distance from Ras-el-Had to Sinai, in a northwest direction, gives the head of the *Persian Gulf.* The same distance, continued in the same direction, marks the *northeast corner of the Mediterranean,* beyond which is *Cape Baba,* the northwest corner of Asia Minor. *Northeast Cape,* or *Cape Severo,* the most northern point of Asia, is on the vertical line A, about one-quarter M below the top.

ISLANDS.—The lines of the approximate figure on the east coast form, as we have seen, four curves. There are, outside of this coast, four other curves formed by the lines of islands, and the two narrow peninsulas. Each of these curves begins above, with a peninsula or an island very near the coast, and joins the one below it, near the middle.

1. *Kamtchatka* and the *Kurile Islands* form the first curve. *Saghalien* and the *Japan Islands* the second.

Corea and the *Loo Choo Islands*, beginning at the second horizontal line, make the third curve.

Formosa, the *Philippine Islands*, and *Borneo*, mark the greatest curve, beginning near the middle of the coast of China, and ending just east of Cape Romania.

A fifth curve, beginning with the *Peninsula of Aliaska*, and continuing by the *Aleutian Islands*, connects the continent of North America with Asia.

2. Besides these lines of islands parallel to the coast, two more must be noted, bounding the Great Archipelago at the southeast of the continent.

One starts from the *Philippine Islands*, and curving to the east, reaches the north coast of the large island of *New Guinea*.

Another, formed by *Sumatra*, *Java*, and several smaller islands, begins west of Cape Romania, opposite the middle of the *Malay Peninsula*, and joins New Guinea, on its southern coast.

These two curves, with that made by the Philippines and Borneo, enclose the great archipelago of *Malaysia*, in the interior of which are the large island of *Celebes* and the group of the *Moluccas*.

CHARACTERISTIC STRUCTURE.

Asia and Europe form one double continent, throughout which is traceable one general plan of structure, though, as in the New World, the two continents differ materially in detail.

Asia is characterized by the immense mass of elevated land which forms the interior of the continent, by a series of great projections along the eastern and southern coasts; a band of islands and narrow peninsulas, in general parallel to the several coasts of the great eastern projections, and enclosing a series of remarkable border seas; and by the distribution of the flowing waters of the continent into many long streams which reach the sea in nearly parallel courses, without much combination.

Western Asia, which may be separated from the main body of the continent by a line passing from the Ural Mountains to the Aral

Sea, and thence to the mouth of the Indus, has a different structure from Eastern Asia, and must be studied separately.

EASTERN ASIA.—From the somewhat square mass of elevated land which forms the centre of the continent, almost uninterrupted slopes descend to the Arctic Ocean on the north; the Pacific on the east; the Indian Ocean on the south; and the Caspian and Aral Seas on the west. The eastern and southern slopes, prolonged in certain portions by outlying mountains or plateau regions, form that wonderful series of projections so characteristic of the continent. Whole countries of vast area are thrust out into the sea, and form, with those belts of islands which owe their existence to the same cause, the most favored regions of Asia.

If we analyze more closely the internal structure of Eastern Asia, we find the central highland region to consist of plateaus bordered and crossed by mountain systems, some of which are the highest on the globe. Four parallel systems, the Himalaya, Kuen-lun, Thian-Shan, and Altai, extend east and west at nearly equal distances one from another. The Himalaya are the highest mountains on the globe. The Kuen-lun and the Karakorum, between the Kuen-lun and the Himalaya, are nearly equal to the latter in elevation.

Examining the profile of Eastern Asia, we find that the entire space between the Himalaya and the Kuen-lun, called Thibet, has an average elevation of not less than 12,000 to 15,000 feet, equal to that of the highest peaks of the Rocky Mountains. Above this elevation peaks rise to the unparalleled height of 27,000, 28,000, and 29,000 feet!

This mountain land of Thibet, continued eastward to the Pacific by the mountains of Southern China, and westward by the Hindoo Koosh, forms the main axis of the continent.

North of the Kuen-lun, the surface of the plateau descends at once, having only from 5,000 to 2,500 feet of elevation. In the west it is interrupted by the high though narrow belt of the Thian-Shan mountains, and the lower ranges north of them; but in the east it extends to the Khingan, and northward to the Altai, without a single mountain range interrupting its even surface.

In the Altai, continued eastward by the Yablonoi Mountains, is again a mountain region, but one of much less extent than that of Thibet, and of comparatively trifling elevation. The highest points are only about 8,000 feet, while the crests of the ranges reach only about 6,000 feet, and the valleys between them scarcely more than 2,000 to 3,000 feet.

This mountain region, together with the Altai, is the minor axis, or secondary highland, of the continent, corresponding to the Atlantic highlands in North America, and to the Brazilian plateau of South America. The depression between Thibet and the Altai region represents in Asia the vast low plains in the interior of the American continents.

Thus we find that the great lines of structure in this continent extend east and west, instead of north and south as in the New World. The outlying ranges which form the great projections, and which are altogether of subordinate rank, both as regards their continuity and their elevation, have, however, a general north and south direction. So do also the Ural and the Soliman mountains, which mark the separation between the two parts of the continent.

Asia again differs from the American continents in the relative position of its extended low plains and its highland regions. In the latter the great and fertile low plains are in the interior of the continent, and the characteristic highland regions are on its borders. In Asia all the great plains are on the borders of the continent, terminating the slopes from the main highlands which are in the centre. This position of the plains exerts a manifest influence on the distribution of the flowing waters of the continent, and causes them to find their way to the sea in long and nearly parallel courses, without much combination.

The eastern slope possesses three streams, the Yang-tse-kiang and Hoang-ho, draining the plains of China, and the Amoor, belonging to the projection of Manchuria. Each of these rivers rivals the Mississippi in length, yet receives comparatively few tributaries. The southern slope also possesses three important streams, the Ganges and Brahmapootra, twin streams like those of China, and the Indus. The Ganges is the only one of these in which there is any considerable combination of tributaries, a fact owing to its position in the broad, open plain between the Himalaya and the plateau of the Deccan.

The peninsula of Indo-China, connecting the eastern and southern slopes, has also three parallel streams of considerable size, draining the main valleys. The Mekong, though occupying a narrow valley, ranks with the rivers of Hindostan, being not less than 1,500 miles in length.

Again, the northwestward slope of the continent, directed to the Arctic Ocean and the inland seas, has also its great streams, in which the general parallelism of direction, and the want of combination, is even more marked than in the eastern streams. Two of secondary length enter the Aral Sea; and three, the Obi, Yenisci, and Lena, which rival in length those of the eastern slope, flow into the Arctic Ocean. These streams are, notwithstanding their size, on account of their position in the Arctic regions, comparatively of trifling value in the continent; while the rivers of China and Hindostan, flowing through fertile plains into a tropical ocean, are unsurpassed in commercial importance.

Again, this arrangement of the plains along the exterior portions of the continent has a most marked effect on their availability to civilized man. The most extended plains of Asia are those terminating the northward and the westward slope of the great interior highlands. The former, by its position in the Arctic regions, is, in part, so cold as to be almost uninhabitable by civilized man; and the latter, by its remoteness from the vast moisture-giving oceans, is partially a desert. Excepting the regions at the foot of the highlands which are cultivated, these plains are, therefore, of necessity, thinly peopled; and the few inhabitants that find a subsistence upon them are in an exceedingly low state of civilization, being at best wandering tribes deriving their subsistence from their herds of horses and cattle, or of reindeer. The plains of China, on the eastward slope, drained by the Yang-tse-kiang and Hoang-ho, and those of Hindostan, on the southward slope, drained by the Ganges and Brahma-pootra, are of comparatively small extent. Both are, however, immediately accessible to the moisture-laden winds of the neighboring oceans, and both are situated in warm latitudes. They are thus abundantly supplied with warmth and moisture ; are among the most fertile, and are by far the most densely peopled regions on the face of the earth ; and have from the earliest periods of history boasted a high state of civilization.

The comparatively low table-lands of the interior, though side by side with China, are however isolated from the sources of moisture by the high mountain barriers that intervene between them and the sea. Though their temperature is such that the vegetation of cool, temperate regions could thrive in all parts, and the sheltered oases at the foot of the Thian-Shan are even adapted to the growth of the vine, yet the larger part of this region produces only a scanty growth of grass, and its very centre is entirely a desert.

This plateau region is therefore unfit for cultivation, and is unable to support more than a very limited population of herdsmen. As the vegetation is sufficient to afford pasture for but a short time in one place, the few inhabitants of this inhospitable region are, like those of the western plains, reduced to constant wandering in search of sustenance for their flocks and herds. They therefore have no opportunity to advance in the arts of civilized life, and these regions must continue to be, as they have been from all time, the abode of a scattered, nomadic, and comparatively uncivilized population. The lower valleys between the Thian-Shan and the west end of the Altai Mountains afford the one only doorway from this vast enclosed plateau region to the surrounding country. Through this, the barbarian Mongol hordes have, at different periods, poured out upon the surrounding nations, carrying dismay and desolation westward even into the heart of Europe, and southward into India. The occasional oases along both sides of the Thian-Shan Mountains, and westward to the Aral Sea, watered and fertilized by the rains which fall upon the mountains and the rivers flowing from them, afford cultivatable regions of greater or less extent. These favored regions are peopled by industrious and peaceful communities, forming little islets of civilization amidst the surrounding waves of barbarism which constantly beat upon and at times overwhelm them. These, with the lower and more sheltered portions of the mountain land of Thibet, are the only portions of Central Eastern Asia that are in any degree civilized,

5

for they are the only ones that are able to afford subsistence to a fixed population.

Under the same parallels of latitude as the desert wastes of Mongolia, and *peopled by the same race,* are the fertile plains of China and the islands of Japan, swarming with millions of busy people, crowded with great cities, boasting a very considerable advancement in the arts and sciences, and a civilization more ancient than that of any other existing nation. Thus we see what immense differences result from a difference in climate, which is in turn due to a simple difference of geographical structure and position.

WESTERN ASIA.—The plateau of Iran, continued westward to the Mediterranean Sea by the mountain and plateau lands of Armenia and Asia Minor, forms the central mass of Western Asia. On each side of this plateau is a depression, beyond which is a secondary highland region, connected by a mountain belt to the central mass.

On the south the depression consists of the plains of the Tigris and Euphrates, and the basin of the Persian Gulf. The outlying highland region is the broad low plateau of Arabia, which is connected with the central mass by the mountains of Syria. The northern depression is in part occupied by the Black and Caspian Seas, while the Caucasus Mountains form the outlying highland connected with the central mass by spurs of the mountain land of Armenia.

This portion of the continent of Asia, together with Hindostan, is occupied by the white race, but we find in the inhabitants of the different portions no less differences in civilization than were before remarked in eastern Asia.

The ancient Hindoos were among the earliest of civilized nations, and among them many of the arts attained a degree of perfection unsurpassed even by the present European nations. The banks of the Ganges and its tributaries are adorned with great cities, centuries old, yet boasting even at the present day a considerable degree of magnificence.

The interior of the plateau of Iran is in general, like Mongolia, a dry, barren region, and is inhabited by nomadic tribes of Afghans, Beloochees, Turks, and Arabs. The mountain regions upon its borders contain, however, many fertile and beautiful valleys, and, particularly in the western portions, cultivable oases of greater or less extent vary the dreary wastes of the interior. All these are occupied by civilized communities, and the middle and western portions of the plateau constitute the once powerful kingdom of Persia.

Asia Minor and Armenia, consisting of mountains and valleys, and surrounded by seas, are much better watered and more fertile, and their inhabitants are more generally civilized. Arabia is a region of steppes and deserts with only occasional cultivable oases, and is almost exclusively occupied by nomadic tribes, among which the Bedouins are most numerous and powerful. Only in the more favored coast regions do we find a settled population with a considerable degree of civilization.

The plains of the Tigris and Euphrates, formerly a region of great fertility, were the seat of the earliest civilization of which history gives us any account. They formed the heart of the great and powerful empires of Assyria and Babylonia, and later of the Medes and Persians, which extended their dominion over all the surrounding lands.

The smaller fertile regions of Asia Minor, Syria, Arabia, and the plateau of Iran, have many of them been the seat of rich and powerful kingdoms, whose inhabitants attained to a high degree of civilization, while the less fertile country around was, as it is at the present day, the home of nomadic people, the scourge and often the destroyers of their peaceful and prosperous neighbors. Thus we find that in former, as at the present day, the civilization of Asia was confined to the comparatively limited fertile regions, while the main body of the continent was almost entirely uncivilized.

EUROPE.

CONSTRUCTION OF THE MAP.

CONSTRUCTION LINES.—1. Draw through the middle of the slate or paper a vertical line, A, the length desired for the height of the map. Divide this line into *four* equal parts, making one part M.

2. Through the top of A, and through each point of division, draw horizontal lines, 1, 2, 3, 4.

FUNDAMENTAL FORM.—1. A little (one-fourth M) above the line 1, and one and three-fourths M to the right of A, mark *Kara Bay*.

2. On the line 4, at a little less than two and one-half M to the right of A, is the east end of the Caucasus, *Cape Apsheron.* Join it to Kara Bay.

3. On the line 4, at two M to the left of A, is the head of the *Bay of Biscay.* Join it to Kara Bay, and to Cape Apsheron. These lines form the triangle which is the fundamental form of the continent.

APPROXIMATE FORM.—*Northern and Western Coasts.*—1. At the top of the line A is *North Cape*, the extreme northern point of the continent.

2. On the slanting line, at one M above its intersection with A, is the mouth of the *Dwina.* Join it to North Cape.

3. On the horizontal line 2, at one M to the left of A, mark *Cape Stadtland.* Join it to North Cape.

4. On the horizontal line 3, at one M to the left of A, is the mouth of the *Weser.* Join it to Cape Stadtland.

5. At two-thirds M above the Bay of Biscay, and a little to the left of it, is *Point St. Matthieu.* Join this to the mouth of the Weser, and to the head of the Bay of Biscay.

Southern Coast.—1. Divide the line extending from A to the Bay of Biscay into *three equal* parts. Draw from the head of the Bay of Biscay to the left, and slanting a little upward, a line equal to one of these parts. At its end is *Cape Finisterre.*

2. Draw from Cape Finisterre southward, a second line of the same length, at right angles to the preceding. Mark at its end *Cape St. Vincent.*

3. Draw to the right from this point another line of the same length, at right angles to the preceding; and mark *Cape de Gata.* Join Cape de Gata to the nearest point of division in the horizontal line. This gives the approximate form of the Spanish Peninsula.

4. At the bottom of the line A, is *Cape Matapan*, the extreme southern point of the continent. Join it to the second point in the horizontal line (*Peninsula of Istria*).

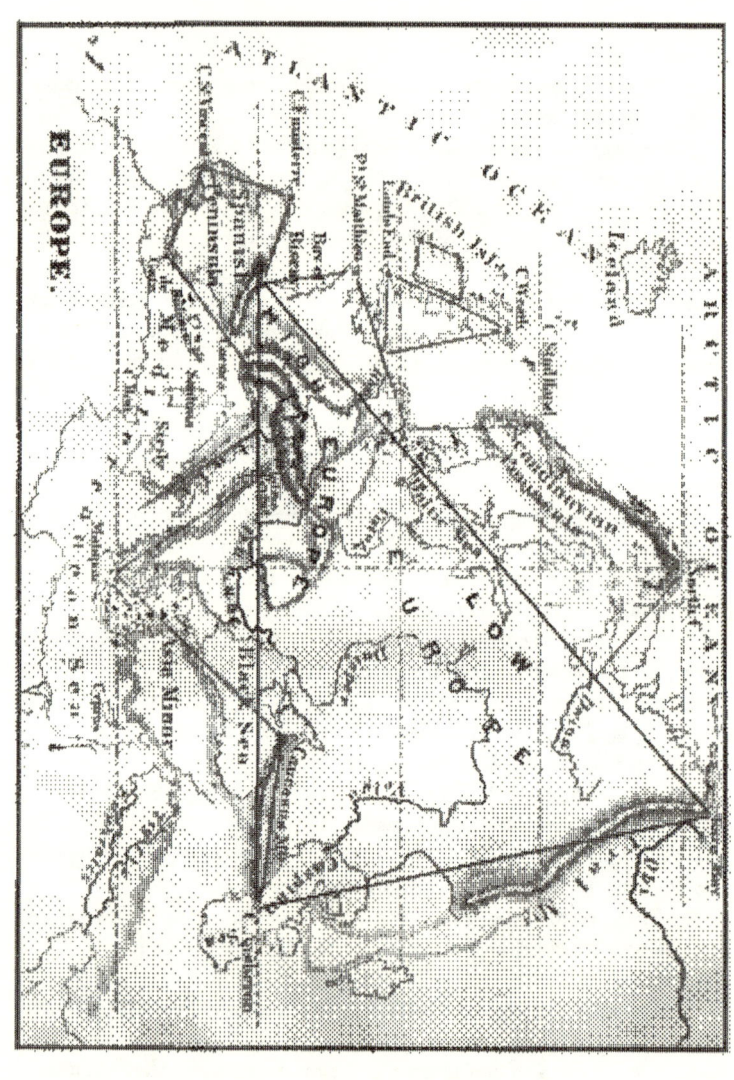

5. At the left of this point, from the middle of the second division, draw a line parallel to the one last drawn, making it a little more than one M in length. This gives the direction and length of Italy.

6. On the lower horizontal line mark a point at one M to the right of A. Draw a line from Cape Matapan through this point, continuing it one-quarter M beyond the horizontal line. At its end is the *west* point of the *Caucasus*. Join this to Cape Apaheron. This completes the approximate form of the continent.

ISLANDS.—The most important islands of Europe lie west of the continent, and are called the *British Isles*. In order to place them, notice that the southeastern point of England nearly touches the middle of the slanting line between the mouth of the Weser and Point St. Matthieu. From this middle point draw a line upward, a little less than one M in length, slanting it a little to the left. At its end mark *Cape Wrath*. From this same middle point draw a horizontal line, and we find, directly above Point St. Matthieu, *Land's End*. This makes the southern base of the triangle. Join Land's End to Cape Wrath. At about one-fourth of the distance from Land's End to Cape Wrath, is the lower end of Ireland. Its figure is a rhomboid, the shorter sides of which are about one-half the length of the shorter side of Great Britain.

The islands of the Mediterranean are very easily placed. *Candia* lies at the south side of the Archipelago; *Cyprus* lies directly east of it, south of Asia Minor, and is about the same size; *Sicily* is between Italy and Cape Bon. *Corsica* and *Sardinia* are west of Italy, and directly south of the Gulf of Genoa. The *Balearic Isles* are parallel with the northeast coast of Spain.

CHARACTERISTIC STRUCTURE.

Europe is characterized by its small size, and the exceeding irregularities of its contour, peninsulas constituting nearly one-third of its entire extent. It resembles Asia in the number and position of southern peninsulas, in the limited combination of its flowing waters, and in the division of the continent into two parts quite unlike in structure.

A line drawn from the mouth of the Weser to that of the Danube, leaves the mountainous portion of the continent, or High Europe, at the southwest; while the region of the plains, or Low Europe, lies northeast of it. In High Europe, as in Asia, the highlands are in the interior, with a belt of plains west, north, and east of them, while their peninsulas prolong them to the south. In Asia, the central mass is the extended and very elevated mountainous plateau of Thibet; while in High Europe it is the mountain system of the Alps. The highlands north of them descend gradually to the low plains which intervene between them and the surrounding seas; while at their southern foot are the low plains of Lombardy, recalling those of Hindostan at the foot of the Himalaya. East of this central mass, consisting of the Alps and their northern highlands, is the plateau of Transylvania, with the low plains of Hungary on the one side, and those of Wallachia on the other. West of the Alps is the central plateau of France, with the valley of the Rhône and Saône on the one hand, and the Atlantic plains on the other. Thus High Europe consists of these three main regions, each of which is prolonged southward by a peninsula; the central with the Alps and Italy; the western with Spain; and the eastern with the Hellenic peninsula. The mass of highlands north of the Alps, as compared with those of Asia, are of exceedingly limited extent, and have the character of mountain ranges rather than of plateaus. These mountain ranges follow two general directions, nearly at right angles the one with the other, and by their intersection divide High Europe into a multitude of small, separate basins and valleys. The Alps and the ranges west of them follow a northeastward direction, while the ranges east of the Alps have a northwestward direction, the same as the Himalaya and the Caucasus. This direction is most distinctly marked by the Transylvanian Alps, the Carpathian, Sudetic, and Harz Mountains, which, with the low ranges that continue them nearly to the North Sea, from the boundary line between High and Low Europe.

Low Europe extends from this border line of highlands, northward to the Arctic Ocean, and eastward to the Ural Mountains and the Caspian Sea, one great plain, without a single mountain range. Its water-shed is a low swell crossing the central portions, of which the Valdai Hills, not more than 1,100 feet in elevation, are the culminating point. The northern slope is directed northwest, like the plains of Asia; while the southern slope is directed southeast toward the interior of the double continent Asia-Europe. At its junction with the Asiatic slope is formed that great depression in which lie the Caspian and Aral Seas.

Around this vast region of plains rise a series of highlands, which border it, and each corner of which is broken by a Mediterranean Sea. On the east are the Ural Mountains and the Caspian Sea; on the south the Caucasus and the border mountains of High Europe, between which lies the Black Sea; on the west and north the Scandinavian highlands, with the Baltic on one side, and the White Sea on the other. This region is, therefore, entirely the opposite of High Europe in structure. The climate of these two regions presents contrasts no less striking. Low Europe has a continental climate, comparatively dry, with cold winters and hot summers. High Europe has a maritime climate, moist, with comparatively little difference between winter and summer. It has also an average annual temperature considerably higher than that of Low Europe.

The difference between the temperature of western Europe and eastern North America becomes fully apparent when we reflect that the plains of Lombardy, with their beautiful vegetation and mild winter, are in the latitude of Montreal, where only the hardy fruits and grains of cool, temperate regions flourish. The great and beautiful capital, Paris, is two degrees higher in latitude than Quebec; and London lies opposite Cape Charles and the frozen wilds of Labrador.

This elevated temperature of High Europe is due, in a great measure, to the southwest winds and currents of the Atlantic, which shed upon its shores the warmth they have preserved from the tropical regions; and its freedom from extremes of heat and cold is increased by its peninsular structure, which allows the equalizing influence of the ocean to reach even into the heart of the continent.

The contrast between Low and High Europe is no less striking in their political geography than in their physical character. Low Europe, one in structure, is also one in race and nationality. Its people, except a few semi-Asiatic tribes in the region of the Caspian and on the Arctic coasts, are of the Slavonic family; and this immense plain, nearly one-half the entire continent, constitutes one state, Russia in Europe. High Europe, on the contrary, consisting of a multitude of small, distinct physical regions, contains a great number of small, separate nationalities. In a few cases a number of these have been combined, thus forming a great and powerful state, as the Empire of Austria. Even in these cases, however, the formerly separate nationalities have retained more or less of their individual characteristics, and can scarcely be said to have become one more than in name. In general, there has been no combination, and each distinct physical region has its distinct state; as shown by the thirty-four small states which constitute Germany proper, and the little kingdoms of Holland and Belgium.

Each southern peninsula has also its separate nation, and has had its special work to perform in the development of European civilization.

The nations of the main body of High Europe consist of two distinct families or races: the Germanic, east of Switzerland and the Rhine; and the Celtic, in France and western Switzerland and Belgium; while still another family is represented by the nations of the south. The British Isles, originally peopled by the Celts, were afterward invaded and permanently occupied by the Saxons, Angles, and other peoples of Germanic origin. In England, the greater portion of which is open country, favorable to the commingling of its various peoples, these different elements have been blended into one, forming the Anglo-Saxon, or English people. In Ireland, and in the mountains of Wales and Scotland, however, where the Celts long successfully resisted the encroachments of their Germanic neighbors, this ancient race, though conquered, still exists, with very little, if any, intermingling of the foreign element; and the ancient Celtic language, or dialects of it, is still employed.

Thus we remark that, throughout the European continent wherever there is unity of structure, there is unity of race and nationality; while a diversity of physical regions is accompanied by a greater or less diversity of race and nationality.

AFRICA.

CONSTRUCTION OF THE MAP.

LINES OF CONSTRUCTION.—1. Draw through the middle of the slate a vertical line, A, the length desired for the map; and divide it into two equal parts.

2. Draw through the top of A the horizontal line B.

3. Draw through the middle of it a horizontal line, C.

GENERAL FORM.—1. At the bottom of the vertical line A, mark *Cape Agulhas.*

2. Divide the upper half of this line into three equal parts, calling one part M (measure).

3. On the horizontal line C, mark a point at two M to the right of the vertical line A; and at one M to the left of A, mark *Cape Lopez.*

4. On the right, draw a slanting line, D, from Cape Agulhas, through the point on C. Continue this line 1¼ M beyond C, and at the end mark *Cape Guardafui.*

5. On the left, draw another line from Cape Agulhas, passing a little to the right of Cape Lopez, and extending a short distance (one-fourth of M) above B. There mark *Cape Spartel.*

6. Connect Cape Spartel and Cape Guardafui, and we have the fundamental or general form of Africa. The north and the east line should be nearly equal.

APPROXIMATE FORM.—1. Outside of this general form there are, besides the great western projection, three lesser ones—one on the southwest; one on the southeast; and one on the north.

2. Half way between Cape Lopez and Cape Agulhas, a short distance outside the west line, mark *Cape Frio.*

3. On the left slanting line, just above Cape Lopez, mark *Bight of Biafra.* Connect Cape Agulhas, Cape Frio, Cape Lopez, and Bight of Biafra.

4. About one and a half M directly to the left of Bight of Biafra, mark *Cape Palmas.*

5*

5. On the line C, mark a point a little more than one-half A to the left of the vertical line. One and a third M directly above this point, mark *Cape Verd*. Its distance from Cape Guardafui is equal to the whole vertical line.

6. Connect Bight of Biafra, Cape Palmas, Cape Verd, and Cape Spartel.

7. About two-thirds M to the left of the top of A, and one-third M above, mark *Cape Bon*.

8. A little to the right, and below the top of A, mark *Cape Sem*. Connect Cape Spartel, Cape Bon, and Cape Sem.

9. Continue the line which joins Cape Bon to Cape Sem, until it is doubled. A little above the end of it, mark the *Gulf of Suez*, which is the head of the *Red Sea*.

10. A little to the right of the intersection of the lines C and D, and one M directly above, mark the south corner of *Gulf of Aden*.

11. Connect the Gulf of Suez, Gulf of Aden, and Cape Guardafui.

12. Draw from the middle of D to the right, so as to form a right angle, a line equal to one-half of M. At its end mark *Mozambique*.

13. Draw from there nearly parallel to D, a line twice M in length, and at its end mark *Cove Rock*.

14. Above Mozambique, on the line D, half way from the middle of D to C, is the most western bend of the coast behind *Zanzibar*. Connect this, Mozambique, Cove Rock, and Cape Agulhas.

We now have the *approximate form* of Africa.

THE TRUE FORM is found by simply joining these points by the proper coast line. If we draw a line across the continent joining the Bight of Biafra and the strait of Bab-el-Mandeb, we shall find the south part to be a triangle with its greatest extent north and south, while the northern part is nearly an oval or egg-shape, with its greatest extent east and west.

The opposite coasts of the Red Sea are nearly parallel to each other, as are also those of the Gulf of Aden.

Madagascar, the only large island of Africa, lies opposite Mozambique, extending in the same direction as the coast of the continent, and its whole length is little over one and one-fourth M.

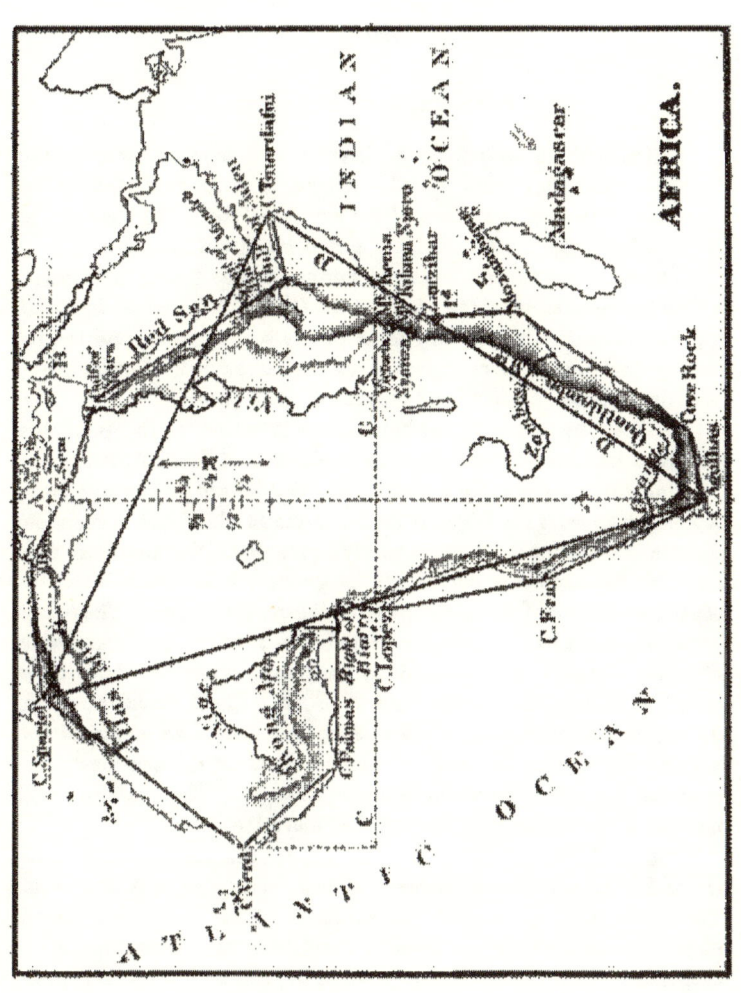

105

CHARACTERISTIC STRUCTURE.

Africa is characterized by its large size, it being, after Asia, the largest of the continents; by the uniformity of its contour; by the elevation of the entire surface of the continent above the level of the sea; and the absence of great, connected mountain systems.

Though three times the size of Europe, Africa has no peninsulas, unless the projection at the south of the Gulf of Aden could be called a peninsula. Neither do any arms of the sea penetrate into the interior; but the whole continent, except a narrow belt of coast lands, is entirely closed against the influence of the oceans.

As seen by the diagram for the construction of the map, the general form of Africa somewhat resembles that of South America. Its plan of structure combines that of the Old World and of the New. A line drawn from the Bight of Biafra to the Strait of Bab-el-Mandeb, divides the continent into two nearly equal parts, the southern having, like the American continents, its greatest extent from north to south; while that of the northern extends from east to west. The southern has the structure of the American continents, two bands or swells of more elevated land parallel to its coasts, while the interior is lower, as seen by the profile from B to B'. These swells, however, do not consist of mountain systems, but are simply an increased elevation of the general surface of these portions of the continent, surmounted by short, irregular mountain ranges. The eastern swell, instead of the western, is the principal elevation.

The northern section of the continent has the plan of structure of the Old World, its bands of elevated land extending east and west. The profile A to A' exhibits its structure. The interior is a broad plateau about 1,500 feet of average elevation, with a depression upon each side. In the western part there is, beyond each of these depressions, an outlying highland region: on the north the Atlas plateau and mountains, and on the south the Kong Mountain.

The southern portion of the continent has a general elevation fully double that of the northern. This elevation is greatest in the extreme south, where the two coast swells unite in the table-land of the Orange River. The eastern swell is prolonged northward nearly

5*

to the Mediterranean coasts by the plateau of Abyssinia, and the low mountains north of it.

The general slope of the continent from south to north is marked by the Nile River, which derives its waters mostly from the eastern swell, and flows northward through more than 30 degrees of latitude. This is the only great stream on the globe flowing from equatorial into temperate regions. The Zambesi, draining the central plateau; the Orange, draining the lands of the Cape of Good Hope; and the Congo, from the middle part of the western swell, all derive their waters from South Africa. The Niger is the only considerable stream belonging to North Africa alone. All these streams, except the Orange, derive their entire supply of water from the middle portions of the continent, between 20° north and 20° south latitude; that is, from the region of the intertropical rains. This region, particularly south of the parallel of Lake Tchad, is covered with a luxuriant tropical vegetation, and is the home of the strongest and noblest animals of the earth.

South of the Zambesi the plateau region is, in the dry season, reduced to a desert; but in the season of the rains is covered with vegetation remarkable for the beauty and the great variety of its species of plants. The mountain and moist coast regions of the lands of the Cape are covered with forests, among which grow almond, chestnut, plum, fig, and orange trees.

From the parallel of Lake Tchad to the Atlas, and from the Atlantic to the Red Sea, the Sahara, or Great Desert, extends across the entire continent. Its southern borders are reached by the tropical rains, and the northern by the winter rains of warm, temperate latitudes; but the interior is nearly rainless, and destitute of vegetation, except in occasional oases, which are in depressions, frequently in the vicinity of mountains.

The Nile, fed by the periodical equatorial rains, overflows its bank for several months each year. It thus stretches a band of verdure across the entire desert region through which it flows to the sea, receiving, for nearly one-half its course, not a single tributary.

The portion of the continent north of the parallel of Lake Tchad, is occupied by the white and by mixed races. The ancient Egyptians in the Nile valley, and the Berbers in the Atlas region, have alone attained to a high degree of civilization. The main body of the continent is the home of the negro or African race proper, who have, except in Soudan, developed no civilization, and even there have but a comparatively low stage of development.

The beautiful valley of the Nile, with the broad delta about its mouth, was the seat of the ancient and powerful kingdom of the Pharaohs. Here, surrounded on all sides by the trackless desert, arose the Egyptian civilization, next to that of the plains of the Tigris and Euphrates, the oldest in the world.

The Atlas region, another fruitful territory of limited extent, fertilized by the winter rains of warm, temperate latitudes, is, like Egypt, isolated from the rest of the continent by the desert. Like Egypt also, it has, by means of its situation on the Mediterranean shores, free communication with the countries of southern Europe and western Asia. Here arose another and more recent civilization, rivalling that of the Roman empire, and, transplanted to southern Spain, adorning Europe with some of her most interesting monuments.

The rest of this great continent, apparently unsuited to the growth of a high civilization within, and, by its structure, barred against the entrance of one from without, has remained, during all the ages of history, silent and unknown. Only in a few favored localities, where modern enterprise has been able to obtain a foothold, and foreign constitutions are able to withstand the influences of its inhospitable climate, is the darkness that has so long shrouded this continent beginning to be dispersed.

AUSTRALIA.

CONSTRUCTION OF THE MAP.

CONSTRUCTION LINES.—1. Draw a horizontal line, the length desired for the width of the map. Divide it into three equal parts, one of which mark M.

2. Draw upward from each end, and from the right-hand point of division, vertical lines, 1, 2, 3.

FUNDAMENTAL FORM.—1. On the line 1, at half M from A, mark *Cape Leeuwin.* One M above, and a little to the left of Cape Leeuwin, mark *Northwest Cape.*

2. In the second line, at two and one-third M above A, mark *Cape York.*

3. On the horizontal line, at about one-fourth M to the right of the vertical line 2, mark *Cape Wilson.*

4. A little to the left of 3, at one M above A, mark *Point Danger.*

5. Join Cape Wilson, Point Danger, Cape York, Northwest Cape, and Cape Leeuwin.

Thus we have the fundamental form of the continent.

APPROXIMATE FORM.—1. Draw a line from Cape Wilson to Northwest Cape; and from Cape Leeuwin to Point Danger. These two lines, below their intersection, give us the southern coast. At the intersection, mark head of the *Australian Bight.*

2. At a little less than half M below Cape Wilson, and a little to the right, mark *South Cape.* Join it to Point Danger.

3. On this line, just above A, is *Cape Howe.*

4. At half M below Cape York, and a little to the left, is the head of the *Gulf of Carpentaria.* Join it to Cape York.

5. A little less than half M from Cape York, near the line leading to Cape Northwest, is *Cape Arnhem.* Join it to the head of the Gulf of Carpentaria.

6. Three-fourths M to the left of Cape York, is *Coburg Peninsula.* Join it to Northwest Cape, and to Cape Arnhem. We now have the approximate form.

ISLANDS.—1. The southern point of *Tasmania,* and its east coast, we already have. Its north coast is equal to the east coast, and parallel to that of the main land.

2. The eastern point of *New Guinea* is about half M east of York Cape. The western point is a little less than half M north of the northwest point of Arnhem Land.

New Zealand is nearly parallel with the eastern coast of the continent. Its northern and southern extremities lie a little farther south than Point Danger and South Cape; and are about as far from the coast as the distance between those two capes.

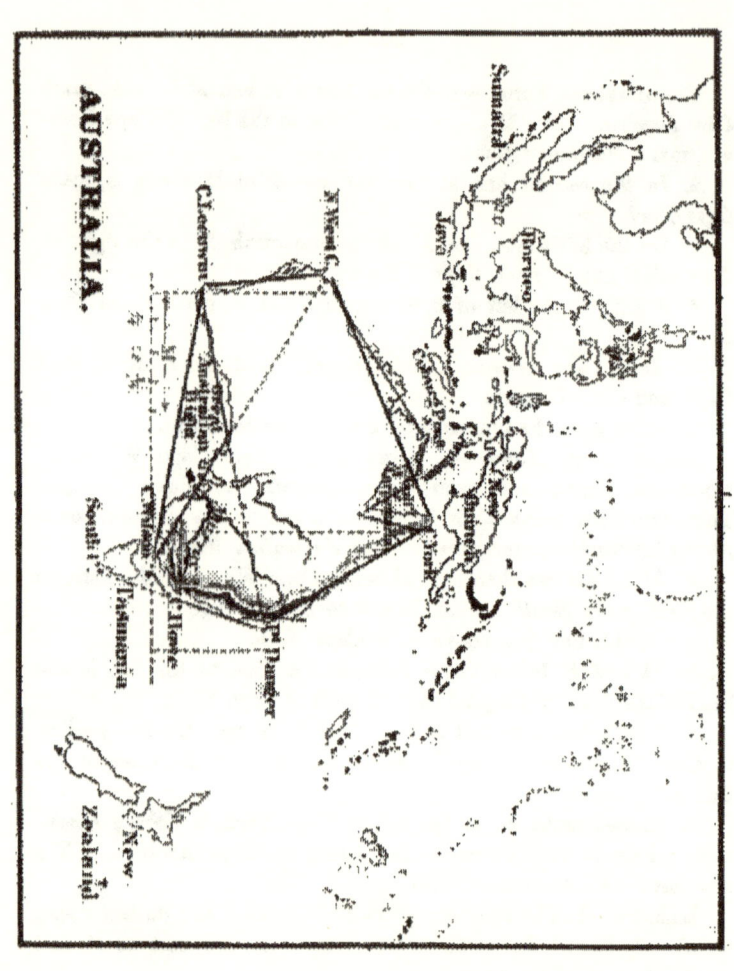

CHARACTERISTIC STRUCTURE.

Australia is characterised by its small size and insular position; its situation in the sub-tropical region, and wholly in the southern hemisphere; and by the simplicity of its internal structure.

The surface of Australia is less varied than that of any other continent. It contains no long or high mountain ranges, and no great plateau.

Like the southern division of Africa, its surface consists of three portions: two swells bordering the eastern and western coasts, and between them a depression.

The eastern swell, as may be seen by the profile, is broader and higher than the western, and upon its southern half rest the highest mountains of the continent. These mountains are only a little higher than the Appalachians of North America. *Mount Hotham*, the highest peak, is about 7,000 feet above the sea-level.

The central depression, as far as known, is a great plain, with occasional small ranges of hills. The lowest portion of this plain is the lake region just north of Spencer's Gulf. Farther north the surface rises gradually, and the land west of the Gulf of Carpentaria, called Arnhem Land, is quite an elevated plateau.

The western swell is slight, and the mountains upon it are low and disconnected. The highest are in the northern part.

The rivers, except the Murray and its tributaries, are small, and, as they have a very irregular supply of water, they are of little importance. Streams which at one time are deep and rapid torrents, at another become entirely dry, or are changed to a line of shallow pools.

The lakes are, in general, salt, and many of them are very shallow. Some are only marshes, and become entirely dry during the long droughts which occur in some years.

This continent, being so near the equator, has in general a very warm climate. The northern part, which is within the tropics, is very hot, and has the wet and dry season of tropical countries. The southern and main part of the continent is cooler, but the change of seasons is very irregular. In some years, there are long droughts, lasting almost the entire year; while in others there are frequent and violent rains during the larger part of it. In general, this part of the continent is somewhat dry, like South Africa and the pampas of South America.

The vegetation and animals of Australia are different from those of any other continent. A great part of the trees and animals are found nowhere on the globe, except in Australia and its islands. The trees have generally small, narrow leaves; and, as they are more separated, and there is little undergrowth of shrubs or vines between them, the forests, instead of being dense and dark, as in most countries, are open and light.

The forests are remarkable for the great number of flowering trees found among them. So far as yet known, there are no very extensive forest regions in Australia. The wooded lands are separated by treeless plains, which are either prairies, or, as in the drier parts, are covered with a thick growth of stunted shrubs.

The country contains scarce any native food-plants, either of the temperate or tropical climates,—a few berries, one kind of chestnut, and a root resembling the potato, being almost the only ones. But the grains, flax, grapes, and other plants of temperate regions, have now been introduced, and grow abundantly; and in some parts sugar-cane and cotton are also successfully cultivated.

Neither are there many native animals which could be made use of by civilized man, either as food or for other purposes. Our domestic animals have, however, been introduced, and succeed perfectly, in particular the sheep, which are now raised in great numbers in all the settled portions of the continent.

The indigenous race of Australia resembles in many respects the African race, and, like them, have developed no civilization. The recent rapid peopling of the continent by foreign immigration is due entirely to the rich stores of gold found in the more favored southeastern portion. The fine agricultural facilities afforded by the basin of the Murray River are now attracting attention, and the settlements, hitherto confined almost entirely to the coast and mountain region, are rapidly advancing into the interior.

Map of the World on Mercator's Projection.

This map is constructed on the supposition that the earth is a cylinder, instead of a sphere.

The meridians being parallel lines instead of convergent, as upon the globe, this map has the disadvantage of representing the lands in the polar regions larger from east to west than they are upon the globe. Thus the form of those continents which extend far toward the poles is considerably distorted.

To correct that distortion to some extent, the degrees of latitude are also gradually increased toward the poles. The advantages which this projection possesses over every other are, that it presents the oceans in their characteristic form and comparative extent, giving the continents their true relative position as seen upon the globe; and that it presents at a single glance the entire surface of the globe, with no arbitrary cuts or divisions, as found in the hemispheric maps. Moreover, the directions toward the various points of the compass being straight and not curved lines, the relative position of the geographical objects is more easily grasped.

As the object of this map is not to study the forms of the continents, but to furnish means for the comparison of their areas and elevation, the forms and area of the oceans, the relative situation of the great land and water masses, the study of the marine currents, the distribution of temperature, &c., the advantages which it presents over ordinary maps of the world in hemispheres more than counterbalances the distortion of form, and renders its use extremely desirable.

The Oceans.—A glance at the oceans causes us to remark at once the broad expanse and somewhat oval form of the Pacific. It is closed from communication with the Arctic, except by the narrow Behring Strait. Hence it is free from the cold currents and drifting masses of ice from the Polar seas, which refrigerate the northern portion of the Atlantic. Again, the Pacific is characterized by bands of continental islands fringing the Asiatic and Australian coasts, and forming along its entire western shores a series of remarkable border seas,: the Behring, Okhotsk, Japan, Yellow and North, and South

China Seas on the Asiatic coast ; and the Arafura, Coral, and New Zealand Seas on the Australian coast.

This ocean is also distinguished by its multitude of oceanic islands. These form a broad band in the tropical waters of the Pacific, extending more than half its entire breadth. The eastern shore presents a strong contrast to the western in the entire absence of large islands and border seas ; while but a single peninsula and one indentation of large size -mark this shore—the Peninsula and Gulf of California.

The Atlantic is distinguished by its narrowness and the parallelism of its shores, which give it the appearance of an immense river flowing between the Old and the New World. Its characteristic form of indentation is that of mediterraneans, or inland seas. Of these it boasts four, the largest on the globe :—on the east, the Mediterranean proper and the Baltic Sea ; on the west, the Gulf of Mexico and Hudson Bay. The Atlantic has also four border seas : the Caribbean Sea and Baffin Bay, which are of great size ; and the smaller Gulf of St. Lawrence and North Sea.

The Indian Ocean is distinguished from the other great oceans by the fact that it extends northward only to the Tropic of Cancer, while the Pacific extends to the Arctic circle, and the Atlantic, with its prolongation, the Arctic, surround the Pole. This ocean is nearly triangular, and its characteristic form of indentation is that of simple bends in the coast line, called gulfs or bays. Two of great size, the so-called Arabian Sea and the Gulf of Bengal, mark its northern terminus. It has also two mediterraneans, the Red Sea and the Persian Gulf, which, though in themselves of considerable size, are small in comparison with those of the Atlantic.

The direction of the principal currents of each of these. three great oceans is indicated by lines of arrows. In the Pacific we find, north of the equator, the north-equatorial current, flowing from east to west. Reaching the Asiatic shores, it is in part deflected northward, and becomes the Japan and the North Pacific current. Finally it is deflected southward by the American shores, and returns toward the equator, to recommence the same journey. The south-equatorial current, reaching the Australian shores, turns in, the main southward, then westward, and finally in part returns northward, along the South American shores, to the equatorial regions.

Between these two equatorial currents is the equatorial countercurrent, flowing from west to east, fed by a part of each equatorial current at its change of direction on striking the eastern shores. Corresponding currents occur in the Atlantic, though, by the narrowness of the ocean in the equatorial regions, and its elongated form, they are more or less modified. Thus the equatorial countercurrent is not apparent, while the northward deflection of the equatorial currents proper is intensified, so that the Gulf Stream is a much more marked phenomenon than the Japan current, its parallel in the Pacific waters. In the Indian Ocean, which has no north basin, the currents present only the main phenomena connected with the southern basin of the other oceans.

The Continents.—For the comparison of the continents, we have their coloring, and the profiles and diagrams, at the bottom of the map. All the continents are here, colored, so that any particular color represents the same elevation in all. Thus the comparative *amount of land* of equal elevation in each continent is at once revealed to the eye.

The profiles enable us to compare the *degree of elevation* of the New World with that of the main mass of the Old World, Asia-Europe; and they exhibit the position of the maximum elevation in each. The profiles are made along the line of the major axis, which in America extends north and south; in Asia-Europe east and west. The general surface elevation is represented in the foreground, while behind are the mountain ranges resting upon this surface, surmounted by their principal peaks.

We are at once struck with the gradual though by no means uninterrupted increase of surface elevation in the New World, from the Arctic shores to the plateau of Bolivia, where the maximum is reached; and the rapid descent from this point to the terminus of the continent. The repetition of the same phenomena in Asia-Europe, but in another direction, is certainly remarkable. From the Atlantic shore we find a constantly increasing elevation of the plateau surfaces until the high mass of Thibet is reached, from which begins a rapid descent to the Pacific. Thus, while each continent has its distinct structure, the two sister continents are in each case inseparably linked by a common plan of structure.

From this major axis there is in each world, as we have already seen, a long and gentle slope on the one side, and on the other a short and rapid descent. In the Old World the long slope in both continents is toward the north, in the New World toward the east. In each continent a major and minor axis are found, running along each opposite coast, with a depression between the two; a fundamental form of structure common to all.

These striking resemblances in the structure of all the continents, and the no less striking differences, which give to each an individual character, lead to the irresistible conviction that there is a general plan according to which each is made with a special form for a special end, while all, working together, are combined in one great organism, which is "the great globe itself."

Diagrams.—A series of diagrams above the profiles furnish means for the comparison of the continents in various aspects. In the first, at the left, the entire area of the continents taken together, is compared with that of the islands and the oceans. The great square enclosing the lesser is the entire surface of the globe, of which the continent forms only about one-fourth, and the islands an exceedingly small fraction, all the remainder being water.

In diagram second, the areas of the several continents are compared one with another, their relative size being precisely that of the several oblong squares.

The series of concentric squares presents the comparative amount of indentation of the several continents. This is usually given in numbers, the number of linear miles of coast for each square mile in the continent being stated. But this statement does not convey a correct idea of the relative amount of indentation and accessibility of the continents compared, except when their size is the same; for the relation of contour to area is changed with every increase of the latter. Thus an area of one square mile, with no indentations or irregularities whatever, must have four miles of contour; while two square miles have but six, instead of eight; four square miles but eight, instead of sixteen. It follows that an area of four square miles requires to be considerably more indented and irregular to give the same proportion of contour to area as an area of but one square mile. To state, therefore, that a certain continent has a given number of miles of coast for one square mile of land, is to give no definite idea of the indentation of its contour, unless the size of the continent is given. The large mass of Asia, for instance, next to Europe the most indented of continents, has only one mile of coast for every 376 square miles of surface; while Australia, next to Africa the least indented of continents, has about one mile of coast for every 357 square miles of surface; a proportion which seems to be more favorable than that of Asia.

To give the length of contour required to surround a given area as one uniform mass without irregularities, and then give the actual length of contour which does enclose it, conveys at once a definite idea of its irregularities, and when traced on paper, affords a ready means of comparing it in this respect with other areas, whether greater or less.

The plan adopted in these diagrams presents to the eye at once the relation of the actual contour of each continent, to that of an equal area, without indentations. The lines enclosing the inner squares, which exhibit the comparative size of the continents, represent the length of coast line required to surround the area of each, were it one unbroken mass; while the lines enclosing the outer squares represent the actual length of coast line. The proportion of the last to the first clearly expresses the amount of indentation. Thus in Europe the contour of the outer square is more than four times that of the inner, the length of the coast line of Europe being more than four times what it would be were the continent without indentations. It is as though an area of one square mile were so irregular in outline, as to have sixteen or seventeen miles of contour instead of four.

Asia and North America are nearly as much indented as Europe, while the three southern continents have a much more regular outline. In Africa and Australia the actual coast line is but little more than is required to surround a square of the same area.

The diagram representing the comparative amount of high and of low land in each continent, needs no explanation.

At the right is a series of squares representing to the eye the comparative density of the population of the several continents, and of the entire globe. The large squares, which are all of equal size, represent an area of one square mile German, being about twenty-one square miles English. The number of small squares included in each represent the average number of inhabitants upon that area in each continent. Thus this area in Australia averages only nine inhabitants; in South America, sixty-four; in North America and Africa, one hundred each, &c. Europe is seen at a glance to be the most densely peopled continent, and Australia the least so.

PRONOUNCING VOCABULARY.

In the following vocabulary, every consonant employed in the pronunciation, except ñ and N, and every vowel not marked in the manner indicated below, has the sound ordinarily given to it in a similar combination in English words.

ā ē ī ō ū are to be pronounced as in *māte, mēte, mīte, mōte, mūte*. ă ĕ ĭ ŏ ŭ are pronounced as in *hat, met, pit, cot, hut*.

AH represents the sound of *a* in *far*; and *aw*, that of *a* in *fall*.

gh is used before *e* and *i* to represent the hard sound of *g*. ñ is pronounced as in cañon (can-yon).

N expresses no sound, is not pronounced at all; but merely indicates the nasal sound of the vowels which immediately precede it. This sound is peculiar to the French language, and occurs invariably when *on, an, en, in,* or *un* terminate a word, or are followed by another syllable beginning with a consonant. The *n* is in such cases silent; and, like N, serves only to indicate the nasal sound of the preceding vowel. This sound is expressed in the pronunciation, thus:

on by awN   an en } by ahN   in by ĭN   un by ŭN

This indicates not *awng, ahng, ŏng,* and *ŭng;* but that the proper English sound of *aw, ah, ĭ,* and *ŭ,* becomes nasal, almost precisely as if pronounced with the nostrils closed. The utterance must be finished sharply, with no vanishing sound. *Toulon* is pronounced, Too-lawN, *Charente*, shă-rahNt, etc.

A.

AALBOURG ; ahl'-borg
AAR ; ahr
ABBEOKUTA ; ab-be-o-koo'-tah
ABBITIBBE ; ab-be-tib'-bee
ABONEY ; ab-o-may'
ABYSSINIA ; ab-is-sin'-e-a
ACAPULCO ; ah-kah-pool'-ko
ACARAI ; ah-kah-rah'-ee
ACCRA ; ak'-krah
ACONCAGUA ; ah-kon-kah'-gwah
ADDA ; ahd'-dah
AD'-E-LAIDE
ADEN ; ah'-dĕn
ADIGE ; ah'-de-ja
ADIRONDACK ; ad-e-ron'-dak
ADOUR ; ah-door'
ADRIANOPLE ; ad'-re-an-o'-pel
ADRIATIC ; ad'-re-at'-ik
AFGHANISTAN ; ahf-gahn'-is-tahn'
AGRAM ; ŏ-grŏm'
AGUJA ; ah-goo'-yah
AGULHAS ; ah-gool'-yahs
AJACCIO ; ah-yaht'-cho
ALABAMA ; al-a-bah'-ma
ALAND ; ah'-land

ALBUQUERQUE ; ahl-boo-kĕr'-ka
ALDAN ; ahl-dahn'
ALEUTIAN ; a-lu'-she-an
ALESSANDRIA ; ahl-es-sahn'-dre-a
ALEXANDRIA
ALGIERS
ALHAMA ; ahl-yah'-kah
ALLIER ; ahl'-le-a'
AL-LE-GHA-NY
ALMADEN ; ahl-mah-dĕn'
AL-PAT-O-KEE
ALTAI ; ahl-tī'
ALTAMAHA ; al'-ta-ma-haw'
ALTON ; awl'-ton
AN'-A-RON
AN-BOY-NA
AMIENS ; am'-e-enz
AMIRANTE ; am-e-rant'
AMOOR ; ah-moor'
AMOY ; ah-moy'
AM'-STER-DAM
ANADYR ; ahn-ah-deer'
ANAM ; ahn-nahm'
ANCONA ; ahn-ko'-nah
AN-DA-MAN
ANDES ; an'-dīz
ANGORA ; ahn-go'-rah

ANGARA; ahn-gah-rah'
AN-TI-COS-TI
ANTISTAN; an-tee'-tam
ANTILLES; ahn-teel'
APENNINES; ap'-en-nine
APPALACHEE; ap-pa-lah'-chee
AP-PA-LA'-CHI-AN
APPALACHICOLA; ap-pa-lah'-cha-co'-la
APOSSON; ahp-sha-ros'
AFURMAO; ah-poo-re-mahk'
ARABIA; ar-a'-be-a
AN-A-FU'-RA
ARAGUAY; ah-rah-gwi'
ARAL; ar'-al
ARARAT; ar'-a-rat
ARCHANGEL; ark-an'-jel
AREQUIPA; ah-ra-kee'-pah
ARGENTINE; ar'-jin-teen
ARICA; ah-ree'-kah
ARIZONA; ar-e-zo'-na
AR-KAN-SAS
ARMENIA; ar-me'-ne-a
ARNEE; arn'-ee
AR-NO
AS-SEM'
ASCENSION; as-sen'-shun
ASHANTEE; ah-shahn-tee'
ASIA; a'-she-a
AS-SIN'-I-BOINE
ASTRAKHAN; ahs-trah-kahn'
ASUNCION; ah-soon'-se-on
ATACAMA; ah-tah-kah'-ma
ATBARA; aht-bah'-rah
ATCHAFALAYA; atch'-a-fa-ll'-a
ATE-A-BAS'-CA
ATH'-ENS
AT-LAN'-TA
AUDE; ode
AUS-TRA'-LI-A
AUS'-TRI-A
AUVERGNE; oh-vairn'
AU SABLE; oh-sah'-bl
AZ'-OF
AZORES; ah-zors'

B.

BABA; bah'-bah
BAB-EL-MANDEB; bahb-el-mahn'-deb
BADEN; bah'-den
BAGDAD, or BAGHDAD; bahg-dahd'
BA-HA'-MA
BAHIA; bah-ee'-ah
BAIKAL; by'-kahl
BA-RO'-NY
BALATON; bah-lo-ton
BA-LEAR'-IC
BALKAN; bahl-kahn'
BALKASH; bahl-kahsh'
BALTIC; bawl'-tik
BANG-KOK
BAN'-GOR
BARATARIA; bar-ra-tah'-re-a
BAR'CA
BARCELONA; bar-sa-lo'-nah
BARNAUL; bar-nowl'
BASEL; bah'-sl
BASSORAH; bah-so'-rah
BA-TA'-VI-A
BATE'-UST

BATON ROUGE; bat'-on-roosh
BAVARIA; ba-va'-re-a
BAYONNE; bah-yonn'
BAYOU LA FOURCHE; by'-oo-la-foorsh'
BEAUFORT; bu'-fort
BEHRING; beer'-ing
BEL-FAST
BELGIUM; bel'-jI-um
BEL-GRADE'
BELLE-ISLE; bel-ile'
BELLUNO; bel-loo'-no
BELOOCHISTAN; bel-oo-chis-tahn'
BENARES; ben-ah'-res
BENGAL; ben-gawl'
BENGUELA; ben-ga'-lah
BENIN; ben-een'
BEN NE-VIS
BENUE; ben-oo-a
BERBERA; ber-a-roo'-rah
BERGEN; ber'-ghen
BER'-LIN
BERMUDAS; ber-moo'-das
BERNE; bern
BES-KI'-DES
BEYROOT; ba'-root
BIAFRA; be-af'-ra
BID-DE-FORD
BISLAYA; be-s-lay'-a
BILUCHA; be-s-loo'-kah
BIRMINGHAM; ber'-ming-am
BIS'-CAY
BO'-DEE
BOGOTA; bo-go-tah'
BOISE, or BOISEE; bwah'-za
BO-HE'-MI-A
BOKHARA; bo-kah'-rah
BO-LIV'-I-A
BOLOGNA; bo-lon'-yah
BO-LOR
BON-BAY
BONIN; bo-neen'
BORDEAUX; bor-do'
BORGU; bor-goo'
BOR'-NE-O
BORN'-HOLM
BORNU; bor'-noo
BOSNA SERAI; bos'-nah se-ri'
BOTH'-NE-A
BOULOGNE; boo-lon'
BRAH MA-POO'-TRA
BRAZIL; brah-zil'
BRAZOS; brah'-zos
BREM'-EN
BRES'-LAU
BREST; brest
BRETAGNE; bre-tan'
BRETON; brit'-ton
BRUSA; broo'-sah
BRUS'-SELS
BUENOS AYRES; bo'-nus a'-ris
BUG; boog
BUKHAREST; bu-ka-rest'
BUR'-MAH

C.

CABES; kahb'-es
CABOOL; kah-bool'
CA'-DIZ
CAEN; kahN

CAIRO; kī'-ro (Egypt), kā'-ro (U. S.)
CALAIS; kal'-is
CALCASIEU; kal'-ka-shu
CAL-CUT'-TA
CALLAO; kahl-lah'-o, almost cal-low'
CALOOSAHATCHIE; ka-loo'-sa-hatch'-ee
CAM-BO'-DI-A
CAM-BRI'-AN
CAM-ER-OON'
CAN-AV'-E-RAL
CAN'-DI-A
CANTABRIAN; kahn-ta'-bre-an
CAN-TON'
CAPE BRETON; brit'-t'n
CARACAS; kah-rah'-kas
CARIBBEAN; kar-ib-be'-an
CARLSRUHE; karls'-roo
CAR-O-LI'-NA
CAR-O-LINE
CAR-PA'-THI-AN
CARPENTARIA; kar-pen-tah'-ree
CAR-TA-GE'-NA
CASH-MERE'
CAS'-PI-AN
CAS'-SEL
CASSIQUIARE; kas-si-ke-ah'-re
CATOCHE; kah-to'-chā
CAT'-TE-GAT
CAUCA; kow'-ka
CAU-CA-SUS
CAYARDE; ki-ahm'-bā
CAY-ENNE'
CEL'-E-BES
CEVENNES; say-ven'
CEYLON; see'-lon
CHAMBERSBURG; chām'-berz-burg
CHAMPLAIN; sham-plān'
CHANDELEUR; shan-de-loor'
CHARENTE; shar-ahNt'
CHAT-TA-HOO-CHEE
CHAT-TA-NOO-GA
CHELIFFE; shel-leef'
CHE-SAW'
CHERBOURG; shār'-boorg
CHES'-A-PEAKE
CHEVOIT; shev'-i-ot
CHICAGO; she-kaw'-go
CHICK-A-SAW'-A
CHIHUAHUA; che-wah'-wah
CHILI; chil'-ē
CHILOE; cheel'o-ā, almost cheel'-way
CHIMBORAZO; chim-bo-rah'-zo
CHOC-TAW-HATCH-EE
CHO-WAN'
CHRISTIANA; chris-te-ah'-na
CHUDLEIGH; chud'-lee
CZNA D'ASTRA; see'-nah das'-tra
CIMONE; che-mo'-nā
CINCINNATI; sin-sin-nah'-te
CLEVE'-LAND
CO-AN'-ZA
COBLENZ; ko'-blents
COCHABAMBA; ko'-chah-bahm'-ba
COLOGNE; ko-lone'
COLORADO; kol-o-rah'-do
COMANA; ko-mah'-na
COM-BA-HEE'
CO'-MO
COM'-O-RIN
COM'-O-RO
CON-CEP'-TION

CONCORD; kong'-kurd
CONCHAS; kon'-kas
CONSHAUGH; kon'-o-maw
CON-GA-REE'
COPENHAGEN; ko-pen-hā'-ghen
COR'-AL
COR-DIL'-LE-RA
CO-RE'-A
CO-REN'-TYN
COR-RI-EN'-TES
COR'-SI-CA
COR'-SO
COUSA; koo'-sa
CREUSE; krews
CRUX; krews
CRIM-E'-A
CUMANA; koo-mah'-nah
CUTCH; kūtch
CUZCO; koos'-ko
CYPRUS; sy'-prus

D.

DAOO; dah'-oo
DAHOMEY; dah-ho-may'
DA-KO'-TA
DANL' KLY
DA-MAS'-CUS
DAN'-UBE
DANZIO; dant'-zig
DARFUR; dar-foor'
DARMSTADT; darm'-staht
DECCAN; dek'-kun
DELAGOA; del-ah-go'-ah
DELAWARE; del'-a-war
DELHI; del'-lee
DEEAVEND; dem-ah-vend'
DEN'-MARK
DES MOINES; dā moin'
DES'-NA
DE-TROIT'
DRAWALAGIRI; da-wol-a-ghar'-ree
DINARIC; de-när'-ic
DNEIPER; nee'-per
DNEISTER; neee'-ter
DONGOLA; dong'-go-la
DORDOGNE; dor-dōn'
DON'-PAT
DOUBS; doobs
DRAVE; drāve
DRESDEN; drez'-den
DRINA; dre'-na
DRUM'-MOND
DUB'-LIN
DUBUQUE; du-book'
DUERO; doo-ā'-ro
DUIDA; dwee'-da
DU'-NA-BERG
DUN-DEE'
DURANGO; du-rahNco'
D'URBAN; dūr'-hahn
DUS'-SEL-DORF
DWINA; dwee'-na

E.

E'-BRO
ECUADOR; ek'-wah-dore
EDELBOUMBE; ej'-kum

120

EDINBURGH; ed-in-bûr'-rûh
EG'-ER
E'-GYPT
EL-AS'-SA
EL'-BA
ELBE; ĕlb
ELSURE; el'-boors'
EL GRAN CHACO; el grahn chah'-ko
EL PASO; el pas'-so
EM'-DEN
ERIE; e'-ree
ERS; ârts
ES-LA
ESSEQUIBO; es-se-kee'-bo
ESPINAÇO; es-poen-yah'-so
ET'-NA
EUPHRATES; u-frā'-teez
EUROPE; u'-rup
EV'-ER-EST
ETAH; air

F.

FALKLAND; fawlk'land
FALSTER; fahl'-ster
FEE'-JEE
FELLATAH; fal-lah'-tah
FERNANDO PO; fer-nahn'-do po'
FEE'-SAN
FINGAL; fing-gawl'
FINISTERRE; fin-is-tair'
FIN'-LAND
FIORD; fe-ord'
FIUME; fee-oo'-ma
FLOR-ENCE
FLOR'-IS
FLOR'-I-DA
FOO-CHOO'
FOS-MO'-SA
FRANK'-FORT, or FRANK'-FURT, on Main
FRA'-ERS
FREDERICIA; fred-er-lah'-ea
FRED'-ER-ICKS-BURG
FRE'-MONT
FRIO; free'-oh
FULDA; fool'-dah
FUNEN; fu'-nen

G.

GAIRD'-NER
GALAPAGOS; gah-lah-pah'-gos
GALATE; gah-lahts'
GA-LE'-NA
GALLINAS; gah-lee'-nas
GALWAY; gawl'-way
GAL'-VES-TON
GAM'-BI-A
GAND, or GHENT; gahnd
GANGES; gan'-jes
GAR'-DA
GARONNE; gah-run'
GASCOGNE; gas-kŏn'
GATA; gah'-tah
GATEBORG; ghet'-burg
GAUSTA FIELD; gows-ta fe'-eld
GE-NE'-VA
GEN'-O-A
GERAL; sha'-rahl

GHENT; see Gand
GIBRALTAR; je-brawl'-tar
GIROOK; jee-hoon'
GILA; hee'-lah
GIL-LO'-LO
GLASGOW; glas'-go
GLOCE'-NER
GLOM'-MEN
GO'-A
GOBI; go'-bee
GON'-DAR
GON-DO-KOR-O
GO-RIN
GOTHA; go'-tah
GOTH'-LAND
GRACIAS; grah'-se-as
GRAN'-FI-AN
GRANADA; grah-nah'-da
GRATZ; grêts
GREENWICH; grin'-idge
GREN'-NAN
GROOS WARDEIN; groce wahr'-dine
GUADALUPE; gwah-dah-loo'-pe
GUADALAQUIVIR; gaw-dahl-kwiv'-er
GUADIANA; gwah-de-ah'-nah
GUARDAFUI; gwar-dahf-wee'
GUATEMALA; gaw-te-mah'-la
GUAVIARE; gwah-ve-ah'-re
GUAYAQUIL; gwi-ah-keel'
GUERNSEY; ghern'-zee
GUIANA, or GUYANA; ghe-ah'-nah
GUINEA; ghin'-nee
GUYANDOTTE; ghi-an-dott'

H.

HADRAMAUT; had-rä-mowt'
HAGUE; haig
HAINAN; hi-nahn'
HAITI; ba'-tee
HAL'-I-FAX
HAM'-BURG
HARDT; harrt
HARZ; harts
HATCH'-IE
HAT'-TE-RAS
HAVANA; hah-vah'-na
HAVRE; hav'-r
HEBRIDES; heb'-rid-eez
HEDJAS; hej'-ahz
HEL-LEN'-IC
HEN-LO'-PEN
HERAT; her-aht'
HERCULANEUM; her-cu-la'-ne-um
HERMANSTADT; hér'-mahn-staht
HIM-A-LAY'-A
HIN'-DOO KOOSH
HIN-DO-STAN'
HI-WAS'-SEE
HOANG-HO; ho-ang'-ho', almost whang-ho
HOLSTEIN; hol'-stine
HOLSTON; hol'-ston
HOLYOKE; hol'-yoke
HONDURAS; hon-doo'-ras
HONG-KONG'
HONOLULU; hon-o-loo'-loe
HOTHAM; hŏth'-am
HOUSATONIC; hoo'-sa-ton'-ik
HUALLAGA; wahl-yah'-gah
HUE; hwâ

HUNGARY; hung'-ga-ry
HYDERABAD; i-der-a-bahd'

L.

ICE'-LAND
I'-DA-HO
IGUASSU; e-gwahs-soo
IL-REN'
IN-DI-GHIR'-KA
IN'-DUS
INNSBRUCK; ins'-brook
I'-O-WA
IPUT; e-poot'
IRAN; e-rahn'
IR-A-WAD'-DY
IRKOUTSK; ir-kootsk'
IN'-TISH
ISERE; e-zair'
ISPAHAN; is-pa-hahn'
IS'-TRI-A
ITABES; e-tahn'-bay
I-TAS'-CA
ITHNEN; e-ta'-nen

J.

JAMAICA; ja-may'-ka
JAPAN; jah-pan
JAPURA; bah-poo'-rah
JAVA; jah'-va
JIHOON; see Oihoon
JITOMER; zhi-to-mer'
JORULLO; ho-rool'-yo
JU-AN' DE FU'-CA
JUB; joob
JUMNA; jum'-nah
JUNIATA; ju-ne-ah'-ta
JURA; joo'-ra

K.

KABENDA; kah-ben'-dah
KAL-A-MA-ZOO'
KAREMA; kah-ra'-ma
KALAHARI; kah-lah-hah'-res
KAMA; kah'-mah
KAMSCHATKA; kam-chaht'-ka
KANIENETE; kam-you'-yets
KANAWHA; ka-naw'-wa
KANDAHAR; kahn-dah-har'
KANEM; kah'-nem
KANKAKEE; kan-kaw'-kee
KAN'-SAS
KARA; kah'-rah
KARAKORUM; kah'-rah-ko'-rum
KARLSKRONA; karls-kroo'-na
KAR-ROO'
KASH-GAR'
KA-TAH'-DIN
KAZAN; kah-zahn'
KEARNEY; ker'-ny
KEDJE; ked'-jeh
KE-LAT'
KENAI; ke-nah'-es
KENIA; ke'-ne-ah
KEW-NE-BEC'
KERGUELEN; kerg'-e-len

KERMAN; ker-mahn'
KE'-ZIL IR'-MAK
KMANIL; kah-meel'
KRANAT; kahn'-at
KHAR-TOON'
KHINGAN; kin-gahn'
KHIVA; kee'-vah
KIACHTA; ke-ah'-tah
KIEL; keel
KIEV; ke-ev'
KILIMA-NJARO; kil-e-mahn-jah-ro'
KINGKITAO; king-ke-tah'-o
KIN-TE-CHING'
KIRGHIS; ker-ghees'
KIT-TA-TIN'-Y
KLAGENFURT; klah'-ghen-foort
KLAUSENBURG; klow'-sen-boorg
KOKAN; ko-kahn'
KOLYMA; ko-le'-mah
KONIGSBURG; ken'-igs-burg
KRONSTADT; kron-staht'
KUBAN; koo-bahn'
KUENLUN; kwen'-loon
KURA; koo'-rah
KUR; koor
KURDISTAN; koor-dis-tahn'
KURILE; koo'-ril

L.

LAALAND; lah'-land
LABRADOR; lab-rah-dorw'
LACCADIVE; lahk'-ka-deev
LADOGA; lah-do'-gah
LAGUNA MADRE; la-goo'-nah mah'-dray
LAHSONS; lah-drons'
LAHORE; lah-hore'
LAIBACH; ly'-bahk
LANGRES; lahN-gr'
LA PAZ; lah pahs'
LA PLATA; lah plah'-tah
LARAMIE; lar'-a-me
LASSA; lahs'-sa
LAU-REN'-TIAN
LEAVENWORTH; lev'-en-wurth
LEEWIN; le'-win
LE-HIGH
LEIPSIC; leep'-sik
LEMBERG; lem'-berg
LENA; la'-nah
LI-BE'-RI-A
LICHTENFELS; lik'-ten-fels
LIMA; lee'-mah
LIN'-ZE-RUK
LIN-PO'-PO
LINDENARE; lern'-dess-ness
LISBON; liz'-bun
LIV'-ER-POOL
LLANOS; l'yah'-nocs
LLANO ESTACADO; l'yah'-no es-ta-kah'-do
LLULLAILLACO; l'yoo-l'yi-l'yah'-ko
LOFODEN; lof-o'-den
LOIRE; lwahr
LOMBARDY; lom'-bar-dy
LONDONDERRY; lun-dun-der'-re
LOO CHOO'
LOS ANGELES; loss an'-jã-les
LOUISIANA; loo-e-ze-ah'-na
LOUISLADE; loo-e-ze-ahd'
LOUISVILLE; loo'-is-ville

LOWELL; lō'-el
LU'BECK
LUBLIN; loob'-lin
LUCERNE; lu-sern'
LUCK-NOW
LUPATA; loo-pah'-tah
LUK-EN-BURG
LUZON; loo-zone'
LY-ON

M.

MACAO; mah-kah'-o, almost mah-cow'
MACASSAR; mah-kahs'-ser
MACKENZIE; mak-ken'-gee
MACON; may'-kun
MAD-A-GAS'-CAR
MADEIRA; ma-dee'-rah
MADRAS; ma-drass'
MADRID; mah-drid'
MAG-A-DOX'-O
MAGALHAENS; mah-gahl-yah'-ens
MAGDALENA; mag-da-lee'-na
MAGELLAN; mah-jel'-lan
MAIN; mane
MAJUMBA; mah-yom'-ba
MALACCA; mah-lak'-ka
MALAR; mä'-lar
MA-LAY'-SI-A
MAL'-DIN
MAL'-MO
MALTA; mawl'-ta
MAN'-CHES-TER
MANCHURIA; man-choo'-ri-a
MANILA; mah-nee'-lah
MANITCH; mah-neetch'
MANITORAN; man-e-to'-ba
MANITOULIN; man-e-too'-lin
MARACAIBO; mah-rah-ki'-bo
MARAJO; mah-rah'-zho
MARAÑON; mah-rahn-yone'
MARETEA; mah-ret'-ea
MARIANNE; mah-re-ann'
MARIATO; mah-re-ah'-to
MARMARA; mar-mah'-ra
MARNE; marn
MAROS; mor-osh'
MAROCCO; mah-roc'-co
MARONY; mah-ro-nee'
MARQUESAS; mar-kay'-sahs
MARSEILLE; mahr-sayl'
MAR-TA-BAN'
MARTINIQUE; mar-te-neek'
MAT-A-GOR'-DA
MATAPAN; mah-tah-pan'
MAT-TA-PO'-NY
MAUCH-CHUNK; mauk-chunk'
MAUL MAIN; mawl mine
MAU-MEE'
MACKEPAS; maw'-re-pah
MAURITIUS; maw-rish'-e-us
MEC'-CA
MECK-LEN-BURG
MEDINA; me-dee'-nah
MEDITERRANEAN; med-e-ter-re'-ne-an
ME-KER'-RIN
MEKONG; ma-kong'
MELBOURNE; mel'-burn
MEN'-EL
MEM-PHRE-MA'-GOG

MESSAN; me-nahn'
MENDOCINO; men-do-see'-no
MENWESTAU; mer-men-to'
MERRIMAC; mer'-re-mak
MESSINA; mes-see'-nah
META; ma'-tah
MEUSE; muse
MIAKO; me-ah'-ko
MILAN; mil'-an
MIAMI; mi-ah'-mee
MICHIGAN; mish'-e-gan
MICH-E-PIC'-TON
MIC-RO-NE'-SI-A
MILO; mee'-lo
MIL-WAU'-KEE
MINDANAO; min-dah-nah'-o
MIN-NE-SO'-TA
MINIWAKAN; me-ne-wah-kahn'
MIS-SIS'-QUI
MIS-SIS-SIP'-PI
MISSOURI; mis-soo'-re
MIS-TAS-SIN'-I
MOBILE; mo-beel'
MOCHA; mon'-kah
MOILLE; m-wahl
MOLDAW; mol'-daw
MO-LUC'-CA
MON-SO'-LE-A
MO-NON-GA-HE'-LA
MON-RO'-VI-A
MONTANA; mon-tah'-na
MONTAUBAN; mon-to-bahn'
MON-TAUK'
MONT BLANC; mawN blahN
MONTE NEGRO; mon-tā nā'-gro
MONTEREY; mon-ter-a'
MON-TE-VID'-E-O
MONTPELIER; mont-peel'-yer
MONTREAL; mont-re-awl'
MORAYA; mo-rah'-ya
MORAY; mur'-ray
MO-RE'-NA
MOR'-TES
MOSCOW; mos'-kō
MOSELLE; mo-zel'
MOZAMBIQUE; mo-zam-beek'
MUNICH; mu'-nik
MUN'-STER
MUR; moor
MYR'-CHI-SON
MURZUK; moor-zook'
MUS-CAT'
MUSKINGUM; mus-king'-gum
MYSORE; mi-zore'

N.

NAGASAKI; nah-ga-sah'-kee
NANKING; nahn-king'
NANLING; nahn-ling'
NANTES; nants
NAN-TUCK'-ET
NARBEV; nah'-rev
NAR-RA-GAN-SET
NASH'-U-A
NATAL; nah-tahl'
NATCHEZ; natch'-iz
NE-BRAS-KA
NECHES; netch'-iz
NECK-AR

NEILGHERRY; neel-gher'-re
NEJD; nej'd
NE-O'-SHO
NEE-BUD'-BA
NEUCHATEL; nush-ah-tel'
NEUSALE; noi'-sahle
NICE; nuce
NEUSIEDLER; noi-seed'-ler
NEVA; nee'-va
NEVADA; nay-vah'-da
NEVADO DE SORATA; nä-vah'-do dä so-rah'-ta
NEVERS; nč-vair'
NEWFOUNDLAND; nu'-fund-land'
NEW HERRNHUT; nu hern'-hoot
NEW ORLEANS; nu or'-le-uns
NGAMI; n'gah'-mee
NIAGARA; ni-ag'-a-rah
NICARAGUA; nik-ar-ah'-gwah
NICE; neece
NIEMEN; nee'-men
NIEUWVELD; ni-uv'-velt'
NIGER; ni'-jer
NIJNI NOVGOROD; nish'-ne nov-go-rod'
NIN'-E-VEH
NING-PO'
NIOBRARAH; nč-o-brah'-ra
NIPH'-ON
NIP'-IS-SING
NISMES; neem
NORFOLK; nor'-fok
NORRKÖPING; nor-chop'-ing
NORWICH (England); nor'-rij
NOR'-WICH; (U. S.)
NOURSE; noors
NOVAIA ZEMLIA; no-vi'-ah sem'-le-ah
NO'-VA SCO'-TIA
NUBIA; noo'-be-ah
NUENCES; nwä'-ces
NUTT'S LAND; nweet's land
NYANSA; ne-ahn'-sa
NY-AS'-SA
NZIGI; nzee'-jee

O.

OAHU; wah'-hoo
OB-DORSK'
OBI; o'-bee
OCEANIA; o-she-ah'-ne-a
OCHULGEN; ok-mul'-ghen
O-CO'-NEE
O'-DER
O-DES'-SA
ORLAND; ob'-land
O'-FEN
OGERCHEE; o-ghe'-chee
OISE; wahs
O-MEE-CHO'-GEE
O-KE-FEN-O'-KEE
OKHOTSK; o-kotsk'
OLDENBURG; öl'-den-burg
OLNEK; o-lä-nek'
OMAHA; o'-ma-haw
OMAN; o-mahn'
ONEGA; o-na'-ga
ONEIDA; o-ni'-da
ONONDAGA; on-on-daw'-ga
ONSLOW; ons'-lö
OOR-TA-NAU'-LA
OPORTO; o-pŏr'-to

OREGON; or'-e-gun
O-RI-NO'-CO
ORIZABA; o-re-zah'-bah
OR'-LE-ANS
O-SAGE'
O'-SEL
OTTAWA; ot'-ta-way
OUSE; ooz
O-ZARK'

P.

PAD'-U-A
PAIS'-LEY
PALEMBANG; pal-em-bahng'
PA-LER'-MO
PALESTINE; pal'-es-tine
PAL'-MAS
PALOS; pah'-loce
PAMLICO; pam'-le-ko
PAMPAS; pahm'-pahs
PA-NUN'-KEY
PANAMA; pah-na-mah'
PANARO; pah-nah'-ro
PAPUA; pah'-poo-a
PARA; pah-rah'
PARAGUAY; pah-rah-gwä'
PARAMARIBO; pär-a-mär'-e-bo
PARANA; pah-rah-nah'
PARANAHYBA; pah-rah-nah-ee'-ba
PARECIS; par-ä-eece'
PARIMA; pah-ree'-na
PAR'-MA
PASCAGOULA; pas-ka-goo'-la
PAS-SA-MA-QUOD'-DY
PATAGONIA; pah-tah-go'-ne-a
PAT'-ER-SON
PECHILI; pä-chee-lee'
PECOS; pä'-koce
PEIPUS; pa'-e-pooce
PE-KING'
PE-LING'
PE-LEW'
PENEDWA; pem'-be-na
PENAS; pen'-yahs
PENINE; pen'-een
PE-NOB'-SCOT
PEN-SA-CO'-LA
PERNAMBUCO; par-nahm'-boo-ko
PER-SEP'-O-LIS
PERU; pe-roo'
PERTH; pent
PETCH'-O-RA
PETROPAULOVSK; pe-tro-pow-lovsk'
PHILIPPINE; fil'-ip-pin
PHILIPPOPOLIS; fil-ip-op'-o-lis
PHOENIX; fe'-nix
PIC ANETHOU; peek ah-nä-too'
PILCOMAYO; pil-ko-my'-o
PIR'-DUB
PISA; pee'-zah
PLAQUEMINE; plak'-meen
PLYMOUTH; plim'-uth
POLYNESIA; pol-e-ne'-she-a
POMERANIA; pom-e-rä'-ne-a
POMPEII; pom-pay'-ee
PON-CHAR-TRAIN'
PONDICHERRY; pom-de-cher'-ry
POPAYAN; po-pah-yahn'
POPOCATAPETL; po-po-kah'-ta-pet'l

Porto Rico; por'-to ree'-ko
Portsmouth; ports'-muth
Portugal; pŏr'-tu-gal
Po'-sen
Po-to'-mac
Potosi; po-to-see'
Poughkeepsie; po-kip'-see
Prague; praig
Prsegel; prz'-ghel
Presburg
Pruet; prip'-et
Prussia; proo'-she-a
Pruth; proot
Pskov; p'skov
Puebla; pweb'-la
Puerta; pwor'-tah
Purus; poo-rooce'
Pyrenees; pir'-en-nees

Q.

Quathlamba; kwaht-lahm'-ba
Cor-neo'
Qui Appelle; kee ap-pell'
Quito; kee'-to

R.

Raab; rahb
Racine; ra-seen'
Radom; rah'-dom
Raleigh; raw'-lee
Ransoom; rahng-goon'
Rap-i-dan'
Rasehmad; rahs-el-hahd'
Reading; red'-ing
Regensburg; ra'-ghens-burg
Reims; reems
Rennes; ren
Re-un'-ion
Reval; rev'-ahl
Reykjavik; rik'-yah-vik
Rhine; rine
Rhone; rohn
Riddy-ope
Richelieu; ree-she-lu'
Rideau; ree-do'
Riesen; ree'-zen
Riga; ree'-gah
Rionamba; ree-o-bahm'-bah
Rio Grande (Texas); ri'-o-grand'
Rio Grande (S. A.); ree-o-grahn'-da
Rio Janeiro; ri'-o ja-nee'-ro
Rio Negro; ree'-o nay'-gro
Ro-a-noke'
Romania; ro-mah'-ne-a
Roraima; ro-ri'-mah
Rot'-ter-dam
Rouen; roo'-en
Rugen; ru'-ghen
Russia; roosh'-e-a
Rustchuk; roos-chook'

S.

Baalb; sah'-lb
Sabine; sah-been'
Saco; saw'-ko

Sac-ra-men'-to
Naghalien; sah-gah-lee'-en
Sag'-i-naw
Saguenay; sagh-a-nay'
Sahama; sah-hah'-mah
Sahara; sah-hah'-rah
Saigon; si-gon'
Saint Albans; sent awl'-bans
Saint Anthony; sent an'-to-ne
Saint Augustine; sent aw'-gus-teen
Saint Bernard; sent ber-nard'
Saint Clair; sent klare'
Saint Croix; sent croy'
Saint Helena; sent hel-ee'-na
Saint Jago; sent jay'-go
Saint Law'-rence
Saint Louis; sent loo'-is
Saint Lucas; sent loo'-kas
Saint Matthieu; sent mat-te-u'
Saint Maurice; sent maw'-riss
Saint Paul de Lo-an'-da
Saint Roque; sent roko'
Saint Vin'-cent
Salado; sah-lah'-do
Sal'-a-mis
Salomon; sol'-o-mon
Sa-lu'-da
Salzburg; sawlts'-burg
Samarkand; sah-mahr-kahnd'
Samoa; sah-mo'-a
San Antonio; sahn ahn-to'-ne-o
San Bernardino; sahn ber-nar-dee'-no
San Diego; sahn de-a'-go
San Domingo; sahn do-ming'-go
San-dos'-ky
Sand'-wich
San Fran-cis'-co
San Joaquin; sahn ho-ah-keen'
San José; sahn ho-say'
San Juan; sahn hoo-ahn'
San Salvador; sahn sahl-vah-dorw'
Santa Cruz; sahn'-tah kroos
Santa Fe; sahn'-ta fay'
San'-ta Mar'-ta
San-tee'
Santiago; san-te-ah'-go
Saone; sone
Sao Paulo; sowN pow'-lo
Sarawak; sah-rah-wahk'
Sah-din'-i-a
Sah-mi-en'-to
Sarthe; sart
Sas-katch'-e-wan
Sava; sah'-vah
Sa-van-nah
Sax'-o-ny
Sayansk; si-ahnsk'
Scan-din-a'-vi-a
Schemnitz; shem'-nits
Schleswig; shles'-vig
Schoodic; skoo'-dik
Schuylkill; skool'-kil
Schwerin; shwa-reen'
Scioto; si-o'-to
Scutari; skoo-tah'-re
Sebastopol; sev-as-to'-pol
Segue; sa'-gra
Seine; sane
Selgheir; selg-gair'
Selvas; sel'-vahs
Sen-e-gam'-bi-a

SENEGAL; sen-e-gawl'
SENETH; se-net'
SEV'-ERN
SEVILLA; se-veel'-yah
SEYCHELLES; sa-sheel'
SHAMO; shah'-mo
SHANGHAI; shang-hi'
SHAN'-NON
SHAS'-TA
SHEN-AN-DO'-AH
SI-AM'
SI-BE'-RI-A
SICILY; sis'-il-e
SID'-RA
SIERRA LEONE; se-er'-ra le-o'-ne
SIERRA MADRE; se-er'-ra mah'-dray
SIERRA MORENA; se-er'-ra mo-ra'-nah
SIERRA NEVADA; se-er'-ra na-vah'-da
SIMOON; se-moon'
SIRHOTA ALIN; se-ko'-ta ah'-leen
SIKIANG; se-ke-ang'
SILISTRIA; se-lis'-tre-a
SINAI; si'-nay
SINDE; sind
SINGAPORE'
SIOUX; si'-oo
SISTOVA; sis-to'-vah
SIT'-KA
SLAG'-SE RACK
SMO-LENSK'
SMYRNA; smer'-na
SNEEUW; snur'-oon
SO'-RAT
SOCOTORA; sok'-o-to-rah
SON'-OM
SOFALA; so-fah'-lah
SOFIISK; so-fee'-essk
SO-KO'-TO
SOMAULI; so-maw'-lee
SONNE; son
SOONGARIA; soon-gah'-re-ah
SOMATA; so-mah'-tah
SOUDAN; soo-dahn'
SOUTHAMPTON; suth-hamp'-ton
SPAR-TEL'
SPITZ-BER'-GEN
SPITZ-KOPF'
SPREE; spray
STADTLAND; staht'-land
STAN'-FA
STANOVOI; stah-no-voy'
STAUNTON; stan'-tun
STOCK'-HOLM
STOLPE; stol'-pe
STRALSUND; strahl'-soont
STRASBURG; strahs'-boor
STUTTGART; stoot'-gart
SUCHONA; soo-ko'-nah
SUCRE; soo'-kra
SUBETIO; soo-det'-ic
SUEZ; soo'-ez
SUIR; shure
SUMATRA; soo-mah'-tra
SURBAWA; soom-baw'-wa
SUN'-DA
SURAT; soo-raht'
SURINAM; soo-re-nam'
SUSQUEHANNA
SUTLEDJ; sut-lej'
SWITZERLAND; swit'-zer-land
STE-NEY

SYR'-A-CUSE
SYRIA; sir'-e-a
SZAMOS; soh-mosh'
SZEGEDIN; seg'-ed-din

T.

TAFILET; tah-fe-let'
TA'-GUS
TAHITI; tah-hee'-tee
TAI-LN-QUAN
TALLAHASSEE; tal-la-has'-see
TAL-LA-POOR'-SA
TAMPICO; tam-pee'-ko
TANANARIVO; tah-nah-nah-ree-voo'
TANGANYIKA; tahn-gahn-ye'-ka
TAOS; tah'-oce
TAPAJOS; tap-pah'-zhoce
TAPALING; tah-pah-ling'
TAR'-NOT
TA SIUE SHAN; tah see'-we-shan
TASMANIA; taz-ma'-ne-a
TAT'-RA
TAU'-RUS
TCHAD; chahd
TOHUCHKEN; chook'-chees
TEHAMA; te-hah'-mah
TEHERAN; te-her-ahn'
TEHUANTEPEC; te-wahn-tah-pek'
TEMESVAR; tem-esh-var'
TENERIFFE; ten-e-rif'
TEN-NES-SEE'
TENGRINOR; ten'-gree-nor
TEREK; ta'-rek
TERRA DEL FUEGO; ter'-ra del fu-e'-go
TEVERE; te'-va-ra
THAMES; tems
THEBES; theeba
THIERS; tice
THIAN SHAN; te-ahn' shan
THIBET; tib'-et
TIBE'-RI-AS
TIF'-LIS
TI'-GRIS
TIE-BUO'-TOO
TIMUR; te-mur'
TINTELLUST; tin-tel-loost
TITICACA; te-te-kah'-kah
TO-BOLSK'
TOCANTINS; to-kahn-teens'
TO-KAY'
TO-LE'-DO
TOM-SIG'-BEE
TOMSK; tawmsk
TONGA; tong'-ga
TONU-KING'
TOR'-RENS
TOULON; too-lawN'
TOULOUSE; too-looz'
TOURS; toor
TOURNEY; toor-ny'
TRANSYLVANIA; tran-sil-vah'-ne-a
TRAVEMSE; trav'-ers
TREB'-I-ZOND
TRIESTE; tree-est'
TRINIDAD; trin-e-dad'
TRIP'-O-LI
TROYES; trwah
TUAREGS; too-a-rigs'
TUCSON; took-son'

TULARE; too-lah'-ree
TUNDJA; toond'-jah
TU'-NIS
TU'-RIN
TURKESTAN; toor'k-es-tahn'

U.

UCAYALI; oo-ki-ah'-le
ULM; oolm
UL'-STER
UM'-BA-GOG
UNAKA; u'-nah-ka
UPERNAVIK; oo'-per-nah'-vik
U'-RAL
URMIA; oor-me'-ah
 or
URUMIAH; oo-roo-me'-ah
URUGUAY; oo-roo-gwi'
UTAH; yoo'-taw
U'-TI-CA
UTRECHT; u'-trekt

V.

VALDAI; vahl'-di
VALENCIA; va-len'-she-a
VAL'-LA-DO-LID'
VALPARAISO; vahl-pah-ri'-so
VANCOUVER; vah-koo'-ver
VARELA; vah-ra'-lah
VARNA; var'-nah
VELIKAIA; va-le-ki'-ah
VENETIA; ven-ee'-she-a
VENEZUELA; ven-ez-wee'-la
VENICE; ven'-iss
VERA CRUZ; vay'-rah kroos
VERMEJO; ver-may'-ho
VER-SIL-LON
VERSAILLES; ver-silz'
VESUVIUS; ve-su'-ve-us
VID'-IN
VIENNA; ve-en'-nah
VILLA RICA; veel'-yah ree'-kah
VIL'-NA
VEN'-TU-LA
VITEBSK; ve-tebsk'
VITERBO; ve-terbo'
VOSGES; vozh

W.

WAAG; vahg
WABASH; waw'-bash
WADAI; wah'-di
WADI DRAA; wah'-dee drah
WARA; waw'-rah
WARASDIN; vah'-rahs-deen
WARGLA; var'-glah

WAR'-SAW
WARTEN; var'-t
WARWICK; war'-rik
WASHITA; wash'-e-taw
WATAUGA; wa-taw'-ga
WATEREE; waw-ter-ee'
WA-TER-LOO'
WEIMAR; vi'-mar
WEIZSACKER; vice-kahg'-er
WESER; ve'-ser
WE'-SER
WEY'-MER
WEYMOUTH; way'-muth
WIN-NE-BA'-GO
WIN'-NI-PEG
WIN'-NI-PE-GOOS
WINNIPISEOGEE; win-nip-pi-sok'-ee
WITCHEEDA; ve-cheg'-dah
WOL-HOV'
WOL-STEN-HOLME'
WOOL-AS-TOOK'
WORCESTER; woos'-ter
WURTEMBURG; wur'-tem-burg
WY-AN-DOT'

X.

XINGU; shing-goo'

Y.

YABLONOI; yah-blo-noy'
YAKUTSK; yah-kootsk'
YANGTSEKIANG; yahng-tse-ke-ahng'
YANK'-TON
YANTELES; yahn-ta'-les
YARKAND; yahr-kahnd'
YAZOO; yah-zoo'
YED'-DO
YENEN; yen'-en
YENISEI; yen-e-sa'-e
YEN'-SO
YORUBA; yo-roo'-bah
YUCATAN; yoo-kah-tahn'
YU'-KON
YURUA; yoo-roo'-ah

Z.

ZAHAR; zi-zahr'
ZAMBESI; zahm-ba'-see
ZANGUEBAR; zang-ga-bar'
ZAN-ZI-BAR'
ZARA; zah-rah'
ZARAGOSA; zah-rah-go'-sah
ZASKIVENNIK; zahsh-e-vairuk'
ZULU; zoo'-loo
ZURICH; zoo'-rik
ZUYDERZEE; zi'-der-zee

INDEX.

PERCE'S MAGNETIC GLOBES.

INDORSEMENT OF THE TEACHERS OF THE CITY OF NEW YORK.

We, the undersigned, Principals of the Public Schools, having used "PERCE'S MAGNETIC GLOBES" for some months in the schools under our charge, do most cordially recommend them as valuable and beautiful auxiliaries in teaching the science of Geography. Principles and Phenomena, heretofore exceeding difficult to explain intelligently to the youthful mind, are made, by the aid of this Globe, so clear that they are readily comprehended by even the youngest pupils.

New York, *February*, 1857.

LAFAYETTE OLNEY, Prin. Male Dept. Ward School No. 14.

OLIVER O'DONNELL, " " " " 1.
N. B. HENDERSON, " " " " 2.
J. L. BOYLE, " " " " 61.
JOHN BOYLE, " " " " 21.
WM. P. BYRNE, " " " " 5.
CHARLES W. LORD, " " " " 3.
J. D. DEMILT, " " " " 1.
ALON. HOPPER, " " " " 1L
JOHN D. ROBINSON, " " " " 17.
L. P. McCORMICK, " Female " " 8.
MARY A. MAHONEY, " " " " 1.
LETITIA MATHEWS, " " " " 61.
MATILDA MOSHER, " " " " 2.
HARRIET M. GOLDY, " " " " 34.
CAROLINE HOPKINS, " " " " 42.
MARIA J. SWEENY, " " " " 21.
CATHARINE WHITE, " " " " 6.
URANIA DOWNS, " " " " 12.
MARY A. DOWNS, " " " " 62.
CLARA M. EDMUNDS, " " " " 22.
C. C. WRAY, " Primary " " 40.
M. C. BROWNBUSH, " " " " 2.
A. N. BEALE, " " " " 11.
HANNAH M. ROUSE, " " " " 61.
CATH. M. CONNOR, " " " " 21.
EMILY A. WHITE, " " " " 4.
M. J. VANDERHOOF, " " " " 15.
FRANCES A. STEVENS, " " " " 63.
LOUISA M. RILEY, " " " " 77.
KATE P. BROWN, " " " " 22.
SARAH E. WHITE, " " " " 61.
MARY McCLOSKEY, " " " " 17.
S. ANNIE McAULY, " " " " 12.
SARAH SMITH, " " School " 8.
MARY E. DUNICAN, " " " " 15.
ANNA C. McHUGH, " " " " 6.
ANNA MAHONEY, " " " " 2.
MARY T. GIBBONS, " " " " 77.
MARY J. KING, " " " " 1.
SARAH E. RAYWOOD, " " " " 62.
KATE A. ROGERS, " " " " 8.
M. LOUISA ROOME, " " " " 12.

PERCE'S MAGNETIC GLOBES.

"This is one of the most beautiful and instru ve pieces of school and household apparatus for the instruction of the young we have yet seen. The Globe being of iron, and the Objects—such as various races of men, lions, Polar bears, steamboats, etc.—being magnetized, the latter adhere to whatever part of the surface they are placed on, and thus not only correctly localize the inhabitants, etc., of each portion of the earth, but satisfactorily present to the child's eye and mind the sphericity of the Globe, and the relative position to each other of the various objects upon its surface. The idea brought before the public by this ingenious invention is a good one."—*Penna. School Journal.*

Patented March 11th, 1864.
By ELBERT PERCE.

STYLES.

Five Inches in Diameter,	Plain Stand,	$ 6.00
" " "	Semi-Meridian,	$ 8.00
Seven Inches in Diameter,	Plain Stand,	$12.00
" " "	Semi-Meridian,	$15.00
" " "	Full Meridian,	$20.00
Twelve Inches in Diameter,	Plain Stand,	$20.00
" " "	Semi-Meridian,	$25.00
" " "	Full Meridian,	$35.00

One Dozen Magnetic Objects, representing men of different races, ships, steamers, light-houses, and various animals, accompany each Globe *without additional cost.*

MRS. SMITH'S GLOBE MANUAL.

Lessons on the Globe, illustrated by Perce's Magnetic Globe and Magnetic Objects. By MARY HOWE SMITH, Teacher of Geography in the Oswego Normal and Training School. 1 vol., 12mo. Price 50 cents.

Extra Magnetic Objects for Perce's Globes.

I. "Animals of all Climates." Elegantly colored, and Mounted on Magnets. 1. Giraffe. 2. American Buffalo or Bison. 3. Camel. 4. Whale. 5. Hippopotamus. 6. Gorilla. 7. Seal. 8. Tiger. 9. Reindeer. 10. Musk-Ox. 11. Llama. 12. Kangaroo. Price, $1.50.

II. "National Flags." Beautifully and correctly colored, and mounted on Magnets. Price $1.50.

These Objects are packed securely in neat paper boxes, and will be sent by mail (POSTAGE PAID), *on receipt of price.*

NATURAL HISTORY.

NOW READY:

NATURAL HISTORY OF ANIMALS

For the Young,

Containing brief Descriptions of all the Animals figured on "TENNEY'S NATURAL HISTORY TABLETS," but complete without the Tablets.

By SANBORN TENNEY AND ABBY A. TENNEY.

Illustrated with Five Hundred Wood Engravings. 1 vol., 12mo, cloth. *Price* $2.00

This little volume is intended to give the young and *all beginners* a clear idea of some of the principal forms in the Animal Kingdom, and thus awaken a love for the further study of Natural History. All the Branches, Classes, Orders, and many of the Families, Genera, and Species of the Animal Kingdom, are described in simple language, and the whole made clear, even to a child, by the Pictorial Illustrations, WHICH EXCEL IN NUMBER AND IN PERFECTION THOSE OF ANY OTHER BOOK *of the size ever published in any country.*

NATURAL HISTORY TABLETS.

By SANBORN TENNEY AND ABBY A. TENNEY.

Five in Number.

No. 1—Mammals; No. 2—Birds; No. 3—Reptiles and Fishes; No. 4—Insects, Crustaceans, and Worms; No. 5—Fishes and Polyps.

Mounted on Muslin, Plain, Price $8.00; *Colored, Price* $10.00.

The above give a good idea of the Animal Kingdom; but, together with the Natural History of Animals, they constitute the most valuable aids to instruct and interest the young in this delightful and useful science. The pictures are the very best specimens of wood engraving, and will challenge the admiration of all for their clearness and beauty. Teachers of Primary Schools, and Schools of a higher grade, will find them just what they have so long needed, to aid them in giving oral lessons; and School Committees will find them among the cheapest and most desirable Pictures which they can buy to adorn the walls of the School-Room. Even to the Professor in the College or the Lecture-Room they will be found of great service, as they afford illustrations of his subject, which heretofore have cost him much time and expense to procure; and for home use parents will find them invaluable for the entertainment and instruction of their children.

www.ingramcontent.com/pod-product-compliance
Lightning Source LLC
Chambersburg PA
CBHW020405030726
47496CB00007B/2312

* 9 7 8 3 7 4 2 8 1 7 5 7 0 *